THE LAWMAN'S DEADLY BARGAIN

LENA DIAZ

INTRIGUE

MIX
Paper | Supporting responsible forestry
FSC® C021394

Recycling programs for this product may not exist in your area

ISBN-13: 978-1-335-69068-5

The Lawman's Deadly Bargain

For questions and comments about the quality of this book, please contact us at CustomerService@Harlequin.com.

Harlequin Enterprises ULC
22 Adelaide St. West, 41st Floor
Toronto, Ontario M5H 4E3, Canada
www.Harlequin.com

HarperCollins Publishers
Macken House, 39/40 Mayor Street Uppe
Dublin 1, D01 C9W8, Ireland
www.HarperCollins.com

Printed in Lithuania

"Are you saying that someone is going to put a hit out on me?" Beau asked.

"I'm saying it's a very real possibility, yes."

"The only people I know of around here who put out hits are the Covington family."

Sierra's lips thinned and she looked away again.

"Well, isn't this just great. If I accept you at your word, I'll have to work with the daughter of a crime boss to try to save my life. If I don't, I'm apparently at the mercy of that same crime boss and his family. I'm damned if I do and damned if I don't."

"We don't know for sure that my family is behind this."

"But you think they are, don't you?"

"Maybe. But you're not the only one in a catch twenty-two here. Once the people behind whatever's going on figure out that I went to you, that I warned you, my life will be in as much jeopardy as yours."

Lena Diaz was born in Kentucky and has also lived in California, Louisiana and Florida, where she now resides with her husband and two children. Before becoming a romantic suspense author, she was a computer programmer. A Romance Writers of America Golden Heart® Award finalist, she has also won the prestigious Daphne du Maurier Award for Excellence in Mystery/Suspense. To get the latest news about Lena, please visit her website, lenadiaz.com.

Books by Lena Diaz

Harlequin Intrigue

A Mystic Lake Mystery

Hunting the Crossbow Killer
Vanished in the Mist
The Lawman's Deadly Bargain

A Tennessee Cold Case Story

Murder on Prescott Mountain
Serial Slayer Cold Case
Shrouded in the Smokies
The Secret She Keeps
Smoky Mountains Graveyard

The Justice Seekers

Cowboy Under Fire
Agent Under Siege
Killer Conspiracy
Deadly Double-Cross

Visit the Author Profile page at Harlequin.com.

CAST OF CHARACTERS

Beau Dawson—Police Chief of the Smoky Mountains town of Mystic Lake, determined to find out whether an apparent accidental drowning was actually a murder.

Sierra Covington—Daughter of a crime boss in Memphis, Tennessee, she travels to Mystic Lake to find out what really happened to her brother, and enlists the police chief's help.

Esteban (Steve) Covington—Sierra's oldest biological brother, whose death she's investigating.

Jake Randolph—Alias used by Esteban the day he was killed. But why was he there in the first place? And who could have killed him?

Rafael Covington—Sierra's second oldest biological brother.

Michael Covington—Head of the Covington crime family. Did he order a hit on his stepson? What lengths will he go to in order to keep his power and keep the police chief of Mystic Lake from finding out the truth?

Chapter One

Beau gripped the long handle of the ax with both hands, then raised it above his head and brought it down with a satisfying *whumpf*, splitting the log in two. He already had more than enough firewood stacked by his shed to get him through the next eastern Tennessee winter and they were only a month into summer. But mindless exercise, pushing himself to the point of exhaustion all day, every day, was the best way he'd discovered to keep from doing the one thing he didn't want to do.

Think.

It was the downtimes, when his body finally gave out and he was forced to sit, that the *what if*s, the regrets came rushing in. Nights were the worst. It was all he could do to survive the long, dark hours before dawn until he could get up and do it all over again.

Run.

Swim.

Chop.

And sometimes, when nothing would drown out the memories, the reprisals, the self-recriminations for even one more minute, he'd pound his fists against the trunk of a tree until his knuckles bled.

Stop it. Don't think. Do.

He raised the ax again and brought it down on the next log,

disintegrating it into kindling that rained down onto the pile of neatly stacked wood.

"Whoa. That was impressive."

He turned at the sound of the feminine voice with a barely noticeable Spanish accent, his hands still gripping the ax's long handle.

A petite young woman with long nearly black hair, wearing a tight black T-shirt and black leather shorts was leaning against a tree about twenty feet away, holding up her hands as if in surrender. "I come in peace." She smiled, the gold hoops in her ears, necklaces and rings on her fingers winking in the sunlight.

He set the ax on top of the woodpile.

"Can I help you?"

"I can wait. Keep chopping wood. I'm thoroughly enjoying all those glistening muscles. Awesome six-pack, by the way. And those well-defined pecs and mouth-watering biceps would make me weak in the knees if I was a weak-in-the-knees kind of girl. You've definitely got it going on."

Frowning at her ridiculousness, he reached for the towel he'd left on a stump. He quickly brushed off the worst of the wood dust and sweat then pulled his discarded T-shirt over his head.

She sighed as if disappointed, drumming her nails against a rose-and-vine tattoo on her right thigh. "You had to ruin the show."

He shook his head in exasperation. "You must be lost. This is private property."

She straightened away from the tree, arching a perfectly plucked eyebrow, her blood-red lips the exact same shade as her surprisingly short but neatly shaped fingernails. "I know exactly where I am, *Chief Dawson*. Or should I call you Beau?"

His senses went on high alert. Who was she? What was

she up to? She looked oddly familiar. But he doubted he could have met someone so over the top sexy with such a brash attitude and forget. So why did he feel as if he should know her?

"I'd prefer that you call me Chief Dawson. Who are you?"

"Not into foreplay, huh? I don't mind if the main course is as good as the package promises it would be."

In his sex-crazed college years, he'd have been tripping over his tongue because of her sexual innuendos. But he was older now, wiser, and knew better than to fall for the fake act she was putting on.

"You need to leave." He started toward her to direct her off his land.

"Wait. Hold on." Her playful mood disappeared and her dark eyes displayed an intelligence and intensity that had been lacking until now. "You asked if you could help me. The answer is *yes*. That's why I'm here."

He positioned himself directly in front of her, subtly looking for weapons in case this was a setup. It wouldn't be the first time a criminal or one of their family members went after a person in law enforcement for revenge over some real or imagined slight.

Her tight outfit didn't leave many possible hiding places for a weapon. But he wasn't letting down his guard. The list of enemies he'd made through the years was long and deadly, one of the downsides to his chosen career.

"Typically people who need help from the police call the station or 911. They don't trespass on the police chief's private property."

"Yeah, well, I'm not typical."

No kidding. "You don't appear to be hurt. You're not glancing over your shoulder as if someone's after you. Why are you here, at my home, instead of at the Mystic Lake police station if you need assistance?"

She hesitated, her teeth tugging at her plump bottom lip.

The sudden rush of his pulse in his ears proved he wasn't as unaffected by her as he'd thought. But all that did was spike his temper and make him more determined to get rid of her. He had things to do, like break open a new bottle of whiskey and watch a rerun of last year's Super Bowl.

"Lady, I don't have time for your games."

"No games. Just some harmless flirting. I really do need your help. But, uh, going to a police station doesn't work for me."

"Why not?"

She remained silent, her almond-shaped eyes glancing away as if she was suddenly unsure of herself. But he didn't believe that. There was nothing shy or nervous about this woman. She was gorgeous and knew it and was obviously used to getting her way by using that beauty as a weapon.

"We're done." He grabbed her arm, once again intending to lead her off his property. His world suddenly tilted as she flipped him over her shoulder. He landed flat on his back.

Ignoring the pain radiating through his body, he kicked out, swiping her legs out from under her, dropping her down on top of him. Before she could recover from her obvious shock, he grabbed her wrists and rolled, pinning her beneath him with her arms above her head.

"Madre de Dios." She stared up at him in wide-eyed surprise. "I guess there's a reason you were the chief of police."

"Were? I'm still the chief."

"You sure about that? What time is it?"

"What difference does that make?"

"The difference between you being the current or former chief. The mayor's holding a secret meeting this morning at your police station. The town council will be there, along with those who will speak for or against you. At the end of the meeting, the mayor and his minions will vote on whether or not to fire you. Smarmy, huh? The mayor put you on administrative leave while the town deals with the Jericho lawsuit and then, while you're home, he tries to get rid of you, permanently, all behind your back."

The dig about the lawsuit hit him hard, threatening to pull him to the dark place he tried to avoid day in and day out by not thinking about it. Careful to keep his expression blank, he considered her claim. He was supposed to meet with the mayor and the town's lawyers early next week to find out whether there was any progress in getting the Jerichos to agree to a settlement. If the mayor was really doing what she'd said, he would have given Beau notice and a chance to speak on his own behalf. Wouldn't he? One of his officers would have notified him, if nothing else. She had to be lying. But why? What did she have to gain?

"If this alleged meeting is a secret, how do you know about it?"

"I have my ways."

"Crystal ball? Tarot cards?"

Her eyes flashed with anger. "Is it my black leather shorts or the tattoos that have you acting like a condescending *gringo*?"

"Who the hell *are* you, *Chiquita*?"

She tried to jerk her arms free, but he held on tight. When she didn't answer, he decided this had gone on long enough. "We're done." He rolled off her, jumped to his feet and headed toward his cabin.

"Hey. Wait." He heard her getting up, followed by the sound of her footsteps as she hurried after him in stilettos, of all things. Not exactly what people normally wore around here. She obviously wasn't used to the rugged terrain of the eastern Tennessee mountains. "We're not finished talking."

"We never really started." He jogged up the steps to his

front porch. "You keep going in circles and still haven't told me your name."

He pushed the door open and half turned to look at her. "I'll call one of my officers and ask about the so-called secret meeting, just for kicks. And you're going to get off my land. If you're still here when I return, I'll arrest you for trespassing."

He stepped inside and started to push the door shut.

"Sierra Covington," she called out. "That's my name."

He froze, alarm bells going off in his head. Was it even possible that she was *the* Sierra Covington? He'd seen pictures of the entire family, many times, as part of official notices from the FBI and other agencies. Was that why she seemed so familiar?

After grabbing his service weapon from the entryway table, he eased the door open halfway, keeping the pistol concealed from view.

She stood at the bottom of the steps, just in front of his police SUV parked out front. Her dark eyes searched his as she waited for his reaction.

"Sierra Covington? Any relation to Michael Covington? As in Memphis-Tennessee-crime-boss Michael Covington?"

"He's my father."

"Aw, hell."

Her eyes narrowed.

He looked past her down the long driveway. It was a good hundred yards to the road out front, with twists and turns surrounded by trees and thick brush. The upside was that no one could see his house from the street. That was also the downside. Someone could be parked out front and he'd never know they were there. Until now, that had never bothered him. Now he was thinking he needed a major security upgrade.

"Where's your Lamborghini?" he asked.

"My what?"

"You're a Covington. I assume you've got a car somewhere, one that costs more than I make in a year."

"Jealous much?"

"More like aggravated that crime does indeed pay, in your case."

"You do realize you're being a judgmental jerk, right? You don't know anything about me."

"I know you didn't walk here from Memphis. Did you come alone, or is your father and a group of thugs waiting just out of sight to ambush me for some reason?"

"Ah. That's what you're worried about. I'm fresh out of thugs today. And my father doesn't know I'm in Mystic Lake. I managed to drive here all by myself. My car's parked on the road out front."

"So you could sneak up the driveway and surprise me?"

She crossed her arms. "I wanted to check out my surroundings, see what was going on before announcing myself."

"You wanted to make sure I was alone." His hand tightened on his pistol grip behind his back.

She rolled her eyes. "Since being placed on administrative leave, you've been up here living like a hermit. If someone was actually here with you, *that* would have been a surprise."

"Who the hell is feeding you information?"

Silence.

He looked down the driveway again, scanning the nearest trees. "If someone is out there playing some kind of shenanigans, planning to jump me…" He pulled the pistol out from behind the door, holding it down by his side but clearly visible. "Don't expect me to go down without taking a good many of you with me."

Her dark gaze fell to the gun before looking up again. "No shenanigans. I'm alone. All I want is to talk. Ten minutes of your time." Then, as if it pained her to say it, she added, "*Por favor.*"

If it wasn't for the note of desperation in her voice, he'd have closed the door right then. But that desperation and the intensity of her expression gave her request a ring of truth. Daughters of powerful crime bosses didn't make a habit of seeking out members of law enforcement. There had to be a compelling reason for her to have driven up in the Smoky Mountains, seemingly alone, standing on a police chief's porch. And the police chief in him was itching to know what that reason was.

Hoping he wasn't making a huge mistake, he tucked his pistol into the waistband of his pants at the small of his back. "I'll have to pat you down for weapons before I let you inside."

Her lips curved in a slow sexy smile, the sly temptress reappearing. "Be as thorough as you'd like, Beau. I promise I won't resist."

He ignored her latest come-on and made quick work of ensuring she didn't have any knives or a gun tucked away somewhere. Even though the contact was quick and as impersonal as possible, his hands practically burned where they touched the generous curves through her clothes. She was dangerous in more ways than one.

When he stepped back, she sighed dramatically, as if disappointed. "Go slower next time. Make it last."

"There won't be a next time."

"I doubt you'll say that when my ten minutes is up."

"I'll give you five. The clock's ticking." He held open the door.

Chapter Two

Sierra stood on the cabin's hardwood floor just inside the front door as the police chief locked it behind them, no doubt still suspicious that she was trying to trick him and that her father's men were waiting outside. She couldn't fault him for that. No doubt he'd heard only bad things about her family.

"Do you mind if I use your restroom?" she asked.

"It's your five minutes. Use it how you want."

She put her hands on her hips. "I told you I need ten. You're not honestly counting a bathroom break as part of my time, are you?"

He gave her what barely passed for a smile as he pulled out his cell phone. "I need to make a call anyway. We'll start the clock when you return."

"Gracias."

"De nada."

She hesitated. "You speak Spanish, or are you throwing out the few phrases you learned in high school?"

"One of my former officers spoke more Spanish than English. I learned enough from him to understand the gist of what he said. But speaking more than a few words, actually holding a conversation, is a skill I haven't mastered." He motioned toward the right side of the cabin. "Bathroom's down the hall, second door on the left."

She headed that way, noting the ranch-style home's layout

as she went. He'd maintained the integrity of its log-cabin exterior here on the inside. The floor, walls, even the ceilings were wood. Tall windows and sliding glass doors off the back flanked a huge stone fireplace and framed a picturesque view of Tennessee's beautiful Smoky Mountains. Her curiosity had her wanting to open all of the doors in the hall to see the rest of the place. But he'd probably toss her out if she did.

Once inside the bathroom, she quickly rid herself of the cheap jewelry she'd donned before coming here and tossed it in the trash. Her research on the internet had shown that Beau Dawson was an incredibly handsome, fit man. She'd made the assumption that accentuating her figure and adorning herself with flashy jewelry and heavy makeup would appeal to him so that he'd be more inclined to listen to her. But he hadn't seemed all that interested. Either she wasn't his type or he didn't care for the gaudy look.

Either way, it no longer mattered. She'd won an audience with him. And she wasn't leaving until he heard her out.

She eyed her reflection in the mirror above the sink. The bright red lipstick and heavy eye makeup really did make her look cheap. Not the kind of image she typically went for, especially since she preferred to blend in rather than draw attention.

After finding a washcloth in the linen cabinet, she soaped it up and went to work removing everything but the barest hint of eye makeup. Breathing a sigh of relief, she tossed the stained cloth in the garbage. He wasn't likely to feel the loss of one washcloth. And she didn't want to risk him tossing it in with the rest of his laundry and ruining anything.

Wishing she had time to grab another outfit from the overnight bag she always kept in her car, she tugged at the T-shirt to try to loosen it. But it still pulled tight across her breasts. Instead, she untucked it, leaving it to hang over her shorts. She no longer looked as if she was ready to cruise the bars looking for a hookup. Well, except for her spike heels. But there was nothing to be done about that right now.

When she returned to the large open main room, his phone was sitting on top of the kitchen island in the front of the house, and he was frowning down at it.

She stopped on the other side. "Did your phone call not go well?"

"It didn't go at all. My officers are too busy to answer and haven't responded to my texts yet." He finally looked up, his eyes widening as his gaze took in the changes to her appearance. A slow smile curved his lips. "Better."

"Thanks." Her face warmed at his admiring look. She motioned toward his phone. "Seems odd that all four of your police officers are too busy to talk to their boss. Kind of makes you think they're afraid to tell you anything until the secret meeting is over."

His eyes narrowed, his expression laced with suspicion. "The daughter of a known mobster travels to a remote mountain town, knows where the chief of police lives, how many officers he has, and claims to have knowledge of a secret meeting at the police station. Give me one good reason not to slap you in handcuffs and haul you down to the station to find out what you're really up to."

"You said I had ten minutes."

"I gave you five." He started a timer on his phone.

She frowned in frustration. "It's hard to concentrate with you watching a timer."

"Four minutes fifty-five seconds."

"Okay, okay. I'll start with this. I'm not a threat to you or anyone else. I'm here to save lives. Including yours."

His gaze shot to hers, his brow furrowing. "Explain."

She pulled out a bar stool. "May I at least sit?"

He sighed and stopped the timer. "Just get on with it."

She let out a ragged breath of relief and sat.

With obvious reluctance, he pulled one of the other bar stools to his side of the island and sat across from her.

"I'm listening," he said. "And I'm not known for my patience."

"No kidding."

His lips twitched as if he wanted to smile. But he didn't give in to the urge.

"I'll try to make this as quick as I can," she said. "My family is a blended one. My mom, Theresa, was Cuban, along with my bio dad, Carlos. We immigrated to America when I was ten and my two brothers were in high school. My dad died of a heart attack a few years later, and Mom did what she could to put food on the table. We had a wonderful life together, still do, except that my mother… Theresa…passed away a few years ago. Cancer."

"I'm sorry for the loss of your parents. I heard you and your mother, especially, were very close—"

"You *heard*? What do you police do, sit around talking about my family when you're bored?"

This time he did smile. "In a way. There are bulletins shared between agencies about ongoing investigations or potentially dangerous situations. It can't be a surprise that some of those bulletins refer to your family."

She grimaced. "I suppose not. But I hate that details like my family's relationships are fodder for the police."

"I can imagine it's not a great feeling. Maybe I can spare you some discomfort and speed this along by telling you what I know about your family's background."

She crossed her arms. "Okay. Let's see what part you get right. Or wrong."

"Fair enough. I believe your mother was working as an exotic dancer when she met your stepfather, Michael Covington."

She stiffened, not sure whether she detected censure in his voice or not. "She did what she could to pay the bills, to feed her kids. It was an honest living, even if people don't approve."

"No judgment here. Just telling you the facts, at least what I've been told. Michael Covington ended up marrying her. It was his third marriage, her second. He had four sons already and adopted you and your two brothers, Esteban and Rafael."

"We don't use the *step* title in my family. Michael is my *father.* And his sons—Thomas, Vincent, Anthony, Charles—they all welcomed us into their home and family as if we were blood-related. They're my brothers and I'm their sister, period."

He crossed his arms on top of the island. "As touchy as you seem about your family, I'll skip all the legal issues your father, and brothers, have been caught up in through the years. Let's get to the part that matters right now. You said you came here because my life, and others' lives, are in danger. Why do you think that? What's going on?"

"To answer, I need to add something else about my family. In addition to being close, we're also extremely private. We try to avoid being in the public eye as much as possible, mainly to avoid harassment by law enforcement. Which is why you might be surprised to learn that my oldest brother, Esteban, died quite some time ago."

His eyes widened. "That *is* a surprise. Last I'd heard he was in Europe managing the family's international crime interests."

"International *business.*"

"Semantics. But let's not get into that. My condolences, again, on another terrible loss for you and your family. That's a lot to have endured."

She nodded her thanks, surprised at the sincerity in his expression, his tone. That wasn't what she'd ever expect from a cop.

"And you're right," he continued. "I had no idea that your brother had died. Are you trying to say his death is the reason that you feel others are in danger?"

"Yes."

"But he lives, lived, in Memphis with the rest of your family, right?"

"All of us live there, within a few miles of my father's home."

"Then what does his death have to do with people being in danger here in Mystic Lake, nearly six hours away? That's what you're saying, right? That his death is somehow tied up with the danger you mentioned?"

She clenched her fists in her lap. "That's exactly what I'm saying."

He shook his head. "I'm lost, unless…how did Esteban die? I'm guessing it wasn't natural causes or you wouldn't have brought it up."

"He drowned. In the lake not far from this very mountain."

"Esteban died in Mystic Lake?"

"Yes."

He slowly shook his head in denial. "Impossible. As the chief of police, I'm aware of every death in town, natural or otherwise. There's no way your brother could have drowned without me being told and my team investigating his death."

"My brother was here under an alias on vacation. According to his friends, they were partying on a boat they'd rented and he fell overboard. He never resurfaced. From what I've learned since then, that's fairly common around here. The town is full of stories and legends about the lake being cursed and spirits holding people under and refusing to give up the dead. My family was devastated when Esteban's friends told us what had happened and that the police couldn't find his body."

"When was this?"

"It's been a little over a year. His alias was—"

"Jake Randolph."

She blinked. "How did you—"

"In spite of what Tanya Jericho's parents believe, the family of a young woman we'd thought had drown until proven wrong, I take every disappearance or death in this town very seriously. My officers and I do everything we can to investigate and get answers for the families. I may not have known that Jake Randolph was an alias for Esteban Covington, but I'm not likely to forget anyone who has gone missing or died here. We did everything we could to find Mr. Randolph. But, as you said, the lake is dangerous and often doesn't return those who disappear under the water. It's why we alert every citizen, every tourist, about the unique dangers and hazards and warn them to wear life vests when they go out on the water. Your brother wasn't wearing one, and unfortunately he paid a high price for that. We tried—I tried—to find him. But we never did. I truly am deeply sorry for your and your family's loss."

The sincerity in his voice, in his eyes, again surprised her. It had her chest tightening with the grief that still tugged at her heart every day, threatening to send her to the dark place she'd only recently managed to crawl out of. She drew a shaky breath. "Thank you. I appreciate that."

He gave her a sad smile. "What is it that you're here to warn me about exactly? Does your father blame me and my team for your brother's death? Has he put a contract out on the police because he's angry that we never recovered your brother's body?"

"His body *was* found."

"I'd know if we'd located a body."

"Not if my family, led by my other biological brother, Rafael, paid a private company to search the lake in secret. It took a long time, mainly because they posed as fishermen and were careful so they didn't bring attention to what they were really doing. But they finally found him and brought him home for a private burial. I'm sure you can understand that my father didn't want any publicity."

"Actually, no. I don't understand. Your brother using an alias on vacation, okay, that makes sense because he didn't want any attention. But why wouldn't his friends, and your family, tell the truth *after* Esteban disappeared? I would have expected your father to bring in resources we in Mystic Lake could never afford and search for his son's body."

"You really can't understand?" She shook her head in exasperation. "What do you honestly think would have happened if my father brought in all of those resources you mentioned and made no secret of the fact that he was searching for his son's body? The media would have been crawling all over this town, making it difficult to even perform the search. And do you honestly believe the Feds wouldn't have jumped at this, opening a new investigation into why my brother was here, why he used an alias, whether some crimes were going on or whatever else they could come up with? We were all dealing with the grief of losing him. Facing all the rest would have made it so much worse."

He sighed. "I see your point. But I wish you or your father had come to me. In spite of what you might have assumed, I would have done everything I could to protect your privacy. No one should have to worry about being bothered by the media, or even other law enforcement agencies, during a time like that. I could have helped ensure the search your people did was expedited and explained away so that it didn't draw the attention you were concerned about." He waved a hand as if waving away his words. "Doesn't matter. You recovered your brother's remains. That's what matters. Although, I'm amazed I never heard about the searches being conducted in spite of the company you used being secretive. How long did the searches last? Or, more to the point, when did they end?"

"Several months before Tanya Jericho was found. When you were looking into that Phantom guy who ended up being a serial killer."

He looked past her toward the back wall of glass, his eyes taking on a haunted look.

"You found her, though," she continued. "Tanya. Alive. You rescued her. And later her parents decided to sue you and the town for not finding their daughter until after she'd been held captive for close to a year. That's when the mayor banished you to your little hideaway up here."

His gaze shot back to her, his eyes darkening with anger. "I banished myself. Until I read that lawsuit, I'd never known the full extent of the horror that had happened to Tanya during her year of captivity. It was… I couldn't—"

His phone buzzed in his pocket. A look of relief crossed his face as he pulled it out, as if he'd literally been saved by the bell. Or, in this case, the buzz. But when he read whatever was on his screen, his expression turned hard, just like at the woodpile earlier.

He stood. "One of my officers finally had a minute to answer my text about the mayor's meeting. He confirmed that there is no meeting. You lied. For all I know, everything you've said since you got here was a lie. What exactly is your angle? What did you hope to gain by coming here?"

She stared at him in growing dismay. "Maybe the officer you spoke to didn't know about the meeting and—"

"He checked with all of my officers, just to be sure. It's time for you to leave, Ms. Covington."

"There really is a meeting. I swear. And it's starting soon. I've got no reason to lie."

"And my officers do?"

She held out her hands in a helpless gesture. "Maybe the mayor threatened them if they told you about it."

"Why would he do that? Our department doesn't have an adversarial relationship with him."

"Even with a multi-million dollar lawsuit in progress, one that was brought specifically because of your handling of the Tanya Jericho case?"

His jaw tightened. "We're definitely done." He reached for her arm.

She hopped off the stool before he could grab her. "Wait. Please."

"For what? You still haven't told me why you think I or anyone else is in danger, or even what you supposedly need from me. You asked for ten minutes. I gave you longer than that. I'm beginning to wonder if your purpose in coming here was to stall for time so whoever is with you could get into place as I left to go down the mountain for this fake meeting."

"No one came with me. My purpose was to warn you about the meeting and to tell you that you're—"

"In danger. Got that. Why am I in danger? And if you truly want me at a meeting you think is happening, what's the reason?"

"Because…because I believe someone may have murdered my brother. I've been trying for months on my own to find out what really happened but haven't gotten anywhere. I need you to help me with my investigation."

He shook his head. "You honestly expect me to believe that the daughter of a mob boss—"

"*Alleged* mob boss."

"The daughter of a mob boss wants the help of a small town police chief to look into her brother's death? A death I already investigated and ruled as an accidental drowning?"

Her face heated. "Now who's lying? You've been reviewing cold cases in Mystic Lake ever since Tanya Jericho was rescued, as if to assure yourself that you didn't make more mistakes. And right before the mayor put you on administrative leave, the one you were looking into was my brother's case. If you truly believed it was an accidental drowning, then why were you reviewing it?"

His face tightened with anger. "Where the hell are you getting your information?"

"*Madre di Dios.* That's what you're worried about? Did you not hear anything I've said? My brother was murdered. You're looking into his case. What kind of person would risk his life to kill the son of Michael Covington and what do you think that person, or persons, would do once they found out the police chief was digging into the case again? If he really was murdered, then you're in danger. Heck, I'm in danger if the killer or killers know I'm looking into the case too, especially if they know I came here to warn you. At this point, I don't even care whether or not you believe me. Just go to town, see what's going on at the police station so you can prove me wrong. But make sure you're prepared for the truth when it hits you in the face."

She rushed around him and hurried out the door before he could stop her. The anger seething inside her had her wanting to kick his police SUV on her way past it. But she resisted the childish urge, mainly to avoid being arrested. Instead, she jogged down his gravel driveway toward the road.

Once in her car, she drew several deep breaths, trying to calm down. Regret was already beginning to weigh heavily on her. Nothing had gone as she'd hoped. But she wasn't giving up. She couldn't. She owed it to her brother to find out what had really happened to him, and who was responsible. And her conscience wasn't going to let her ignore that Beau Dawson reopening her brother's case could lead to lethal consequences for him. She fervently hoped that she'd at least made him curious enough to actually go to the police station. Seeing what was going on would go a long way toward getting him to trust her and to take the danger to himself seriously.

Sometimes she wished she didn't care what happened to other people. It could be incredibly inconvenient and frustrating.

She took her phone and opened the app she'd loaded a week earlier. When she clicked on one of the icons, a picture filled the screen. She let out a relieved breath. At least one thing had gone right. Her clumsy placement of the tiny camera under the edge of the hallway table as she was leaving showed an excellent, though slightly tilted, view of the entryway in the chief's home. If she'd had more time, she'd have managed something more sophisticated, with sound.

Like the cameras she'd put in the mayor's office and the police station.

Chapter Three

After a quick shower to slough off the dust and sweat from chopping wood, Beau headed down the mountain. Not because he believed there was a secret meeting about to happen but because he needed to warn his officers that the town was under the scrutiny of the Covingtons. If Sierra's claims about her brother's death were true, it was possible she was right that he and others were in danger. Reopening an old case wouldn't exactly make the killer or killers happy. And, as she'd said, if they would dare to kill her brother, they'd think nothing of killing some small town cops.

The pain in Sierra's eyes and the grief in her voice as she'd told him about her brother had certainly seemed genuine. But once he'd received that text, and knew she'd lied about the meeting, he couldn't risk trusting her. About anything. Instead, he'd look into her claims and find out the truth for himself. No matter what, he had to remember she was a crime boss's daughter. Nothing she said could be taken at face value, no matter how much her apparent grief had tugged at him, making him long to pull her into his arms and comfort her.

He shook his head at that ridiculous thought and left his police SUV parked in the lot at the end of Main Street, then headed up the seldom-used alley behind the police station. It felt odd not using the front door. But there was a tiny sliver of doubt remaining about the supposed meeting. While he couldn't imagine his team lying to him, he also couldn't think of a reason for Sierra to lie about there being one, not when he could easily prove or disprove what she'd said. And to do that, he preferred to scout out the situation in the police station before announcing his presence.

He unlocked the back door, then eased it open, peering down the short hallway to make sure he didn't see anyone before stepping inside. He quietly shut and locked the door, then stood with his back to the wall to assess the situation. It only took a few minutes of eavesdropping to realize that Sierra wasn't the one who'd lied about the meeting. His team was.

He could clearly hear the meeting taking place in the open area of the station just beyond the hallway, what they referred to as the *squad room* in their tiny police station. And he recognized every voice that spoke. They were discussing the fate of his job as the chief of police.

Just like Sierra had told him.

He tamped down his guilt over how he'd treated her and focused on the debate going on just outside of his field of vision.

"This Phil Gunther guy who abducted Tanya Jericho, he was known as the Phantom," the mayor said. "He was living up in the mountains for years. Decades. There were reports of burglaries in people's vacation cabins during that time, off and on. From what we've found out since all of this came to light, some of those burglaries were him breaking in and living in those cabins and taking the supplies while the owners were out of state. Officer Fletcher, you were in charge of a lot of those types of investigations. Were any of them actually solved at the time?"

"Yes, sir. Most of them were. Quite a few were from local teens, breaking in out of boredom or on a dare."

"But some went unsolved, correct?"

"Well, yes, but not that many."

"How many? I told you to check the records prior to this meeting. What did you find?"

"I, uh, a couple here and there. We have an excellent solve rate for crimes in Mystic Lake. It's the, ah, disappearances that often go cold. And of course that's mainly because of the lake, the hazards under the water that—"

"Officer Fletcher, what is the exact number of similar unsolved cabin break-ins and burglaries?"

She cleared her throat. "Two to three per year."

"For how long? As long as Chief Dawson has been the chief of police? That long?"

She mumbled a reply.

"What was that?" the mayor said. "Speak up."

She sighed. "Yes. Two to three per year went unsolved, pretty much every year as far back as I could find records."

"Thank you, Officer Fletcher," the mayor said. "Two per year is a pattern. The chief should have realized that and investigated to determine why that pattern existed. If he had, he might have figured out that there was someone living up in the mountains, off the radar, breaking into cabins to get supplies. And if he'd followed through, this Phantom could have been caught years ago, preventing many deaths blamed on the so-called ghosts of Mystic Lake."

"Mr. Mayor." This time it was Officer Collier who spoke up. "That's not a fair conclusion. None of us officers ever connected those break-ins. And even if we had, who's to say we could have figured out there was one person behind those crimes, let alone catch him?"

"Your chief is the one responsible for analyzing crime statistics for the department. Even if none of you noticed what was actually going on, he should have."

"May I speak please, Mr. Mayor?" Lydia Jericho's pain-filled voice cut through their arguments.

Beau winced. The last time he'd spoken to her and her husband was about two months ago at the hospital in Chattanooga where their daughter, Tanya, was being treated. The young girl had been abducted when she was fifteen and kept captive for nearly a year by the Phantom.

Beau had been just as involved in the investigation into Tanya's disappearance as his officers. And he'd come to the conclusion that she must have drowned in Mystic Lake. It wasn't until an outside investigator came to town that the truth was revealed: Tanya was alive and had been suffering at the hands of a psychopath the entire time.

Beau shook himself from his morose thoughts and focused on what Mrs. Jericho was saying.

"He told us that she was gone. That our little girl had drowned in the lake. And all that time she was up in those mountains, being tortured and…" Her voice broke.

"Take your time, sweetheart." Her husband comforted her.

The guilt and self-recriminations that Beau had been struggling with ever since Tanya was rescued came rushing back with a vengeance. He ran a shaking hand through his short hair.

Images of Tanya after she'd been found whirled around in his mind like a kaleidoscope. Her long red hair, matted and dirty. Her clothes tattered and torn. She was painfully thin, ghostly pale from being kept so much of the time in a homemade jail cell in a cave. But it was the look in her eyes that Beau would never forget. There was no joy at being rescued, no smiles for her parents when she was reunited with them at the hospital. There was only…emptiness, a vacant stare that spoke of trauma that none of them could ever begin to imagine or understand.

Trauma that Beau might have prevented or at least cut short if he'd kept looking for her.

The awkward silence was broken by the sound of a throat clearing. Then Tanya's mother continued, echoing Beau's own thoughts.

"If Chief Dawson had kept investigating, if he hadn't let the case go cold, maybe she'd have been found earlier. The truth is that the only reason our little girl was found alive was because her school teacher kept pushing the case forward by bringing in help from outsiders. If she hadn't done that, the case never would have been solved. Tanya would have died in those mountains. And that monster would still be sneaking around our town, abducting and hurting others. What else do you need to know besides that? He's incompetent. He needs to go. Her father and I will agree to the settlement you've offered, as discussed, but only if our proposed condition is agreed to, that Chief Dawson is fired."

Beau hung his head as the discussion in the squad room became heated. It became hard to distinguish who was saying what, but there was no doubt where the mayor stood on the issue.

He wanted to fire Beau.

When one of Beau's officers spoke up again to defend him, he straightened away from the wall. He couldn't stand here any longer while those under his command risked their own careers and livelihoods on his behalf. It was time to end this.

He rounded the corner and entered the squad room. Everyone went quiet, and every eye turned toward him.

The mayor's shocked expression would have been comical at any other time. But the pain on Lydia Jericho's pale face as she stared at him was nothing to laugh at.

Ignoring the mayor, the lawyers, and everyone else in the room, Beau crossed the short distance to where the Jerichos were seated. Raymond Jericho put a protective arm around his wife's shoulders as they both looked up at Beau.

"Mr. Jericho, Mrs. Jericho, I'm so sorry that I failed you and your daughter. If I could go back in time and—"

Mrs. Jericho stood and slapped him hard across the face.

A collective gasp went up around the room. Mr. Jericho jumped to his feet and put his arm around his wife again, his face turning red as he apologized for her actions.

The burning in Beau's cheek was nothing compared to the guilt slamming through him. "The only one who owes anyone an apology is me. I'm truly, deeply sorry that my actions, or inactions, hurt Tanya and your family."

If Mr. Jericho hadn't been holding onto his wife, Beau was certain she'd have slapped him again. But no amount of physical pain she could inflict could hurt him more than seeing the hurt and loathing in her eyes as she glared at him.

Knowing that nothing he could say would ever make it right, he did the only thing he could to try to atone for his sins. He strode to the desk where the mayor and lawyers were sitting and set his badge in front of them. He popped the magazine out of his police-issued firearm and cleared the round from the chamber, then set the empty gun beside his badge. Lastly, he took the key fob for the police SUV he'd driven here off his key chain and tossed it onto the desk.

"Chief," one of his officers, Liza Fletcher, called out. "None of this is your fault." She gave the mayor a defiant look then faced Tanya's parents. "Mrs. Jericho, we're all so very sorry for what Tanya suffered. But the person responsible for that is Phil Gunther, not Chief Dawson. What you just did is wrong. And, frankly, it's assault." She reached for the handcuffs on her utility belt.

"Don't." Beau shook his head at her.

He could see the struggle going on inside her. But her respect for him as her boss won out, and she dropped her hands to her sides.

He scanned the faces of his officers. "I'm still the chief of police. And I'm ordering all of you—Collier, Fletcher, O'Brien, Ortiz—not to pursue this any further. Let it go."

He turned back to the mayor. "Nothing to do with the Phantom investigation is anyone's responsibility but mine. As the chief, both the successes and the failures of my department fall on me. There's no need to take a vote on whether or not to fire me. I quit."

Beau ignored the chaos that erupted around him and headed out the front door. As he began the long walk home, the sound of footsteps running behind him had him swearing and turning around.

Officer Chris Collier stopped a few feet away, his face red with anger. "Chief, don't you dare give up. Don't let that coward mayor take the easy way out just to avoid a lawsuit. The city has insurance for this type of thing. It will be okay. Come back inside and—"

"I'm not the chief anymore, Collier. It's over."

"No. It's not. I guarantee that most, if not all, of the council is in there right now telling the mayor to refuse your resignation. Your other officers are arguing right along with them. We…we couldn't tell you about the meeting. We were ordered, threatened actually, not to. But we're not going to back off from this. You're the best chief this town has ever had. You've done a ton of good and—"

Beau put his hand on Collier's shoulder, stopping him. "I appreciate what you and the others are trying to do. But I've made my decision. Honestly, I was leaning toward resigning even before I found out about the meeting. Hearing the mayor's arguments and Tanya's mother simply helped me make up my mind. Go on, Collier. Go back inside and tell the other officers it's over. Don't get on the mayor's bad side. Save your own jobs. I don't need or want you to save mine."

"But, sir—"

"Good-bye, Collier." Beau turned around and started down the sidewalk again. Several moments passed before he finally heard the sound of Collier's footsteps receding as he headed back to the police station. Beau passed the parking lot, then the lake where it ended here in town, and headed toward the long winding gravel road up the mountain that would take him home.

Relief that no one was trying to stop him anymore had his shoulders relaxing. He didn't want any of the people he'd worked with to get in trouble because of him. He could weather the loss of his job without any immediate difficulty. Beau wasn't exactly wealthy. But he wasn't hurting either. He'd made sound investments over the years and would be okay for a good long while before he'd be forced to enter the job market again.

The question was what kind of job that might be.

Ever since he was a kid, he'd wanted to be a police officer. And while he had plenty of law enforcement contacts in the state that he could tap to get a job in another town or county, he wasn't sure he wanted to be in law enforcement anymore. Maybe today's meeting was his wake-up call that it was time to do something else, something where the stakes weren't life-or-death and he couldn't hurt anyone if he made a bad decision.

Like the decision he'd made to leave that meeting.

He should have stayed. He realized that now. Not to argue on his own behalf or even to stick around for a meaningless vote, but to do what he'd intended to do when he'd headed downtown. He should have told his officers about the visit from Sierra Covington. They needed to begin an investigation into how she knew what she did and whether others, like her father's henchmen, were also in town. He'd call and warn his officers after he got home.

The sound of tires slowly crunching on gravel had him sighing. Collier or one of the others must have decided to try again to change his mind. He kept walking as the car pulled up alongside him, creeping along to match his pace.

When he finally looked over, he didn't recognize the vehicle. It was a banged-up black four-wheel drive Jeep Wrangler that had seen far better days.

The passenger window rolled down and a familiar face looked back at him, wearing a blue plaid shirt this time instead of a tight black T-shirt. "Hey, stranger. How do you like my Lamborghini?"

He reluctantly smiled. "I might have made some inaccurate assumptions earlier."

"Is that an apology?"

"Don't push it, Covington."

"I take it things didn't go the way you would have preferred?"

"At the secret meeting you somehow knew about?"

"Um, yes."

He sighed.

She hesitated, then asked, "Did they fire you?"

"I didn't give them a chance. I quit." He continued his slow, steady walk up the steep narrow road with the Jeep keeping pace beside him.

"I thought you would have put up more of a fight."

He stopped, and the Jeep jerked to a halt. Beau rested his forearms in the window opening of the passenger door. "*More* of a fight? How would you know what I did or didn't do?"

Her eyes widened. "Um, I don't of course. I just, I mean, you haven't been gone all that long, and I thought you must have given up rather quickly."

"You're lying. You knew I didn't fight at all. If this was anywhere else but Mystic Lake, I'd suspect one of my officers was spying for you. But I know my people. I'd trust them with my life. There's only one other way I can think of that you got your information. You've somehow put a hidden camera inside the police station, haven't you? Let me guess. There's one at the mayor's office too."

Her lips compressed in a tight line.

Beau started laughing. "I knew it."

She stared at him in surprise. "You're not angry? You're not going to threaten to arrest me?"

His smile faded. "I should be furious. But what would have been a huge deal to me an hour ago isn't scoring very high on my give-a-care meter today. Plus, I no longer have the authority to arrest you." He gave her a stern look. "You will have the cameras removed, though, right? Promise me or I'll call someone who *can* arrest you."

"You'd believe me if I give you my word?"

"Hell no. But I owe you one for alerting me about the meeting. I'll give you a chance to correct your mistake and remove the cameras before someone finds them. Then I'll phone in an anonymous tip about someone potentially bugging the police station and mayor's office, to make sure you followed through. How much time will you need before I send in that tip?"

She sighed. "A week? I still might glean more useful information from my cameras."

"You've got twenty-four hours, not a minute more."

"You and your deadlines. It's annoying."

"That needle on my don't-care meter isn't even budging." He started walking again.

The Jeep quickly caught up and slowed beside him. "It's a long walk home, Beau. If you're not afraid of tarnishing your reputation by being seen with a Covington, I'm happy to give you a lift."

He let out a deep breath and stopped. "I'm not particularly concerned with my reputation right now." He rested his forearms in the window opening again. "What's your end game? What exactly do you want from me? I'm no longer in a position of power to help you access police files about your brother's case."

"You could call me Sierra, for one."

"And?"

"I still want to work with you on my brother's case. You know more about it than anyone else, especially since you recently reopened it. And until we know who killed him—"

"If he was actually murdered."

"If," she agreed. "But if he was, the killer likely has you on his radar. All it took for me to find out that you were reexamining cold cases, including my brother's, was to overhear conversations at nearby tables in a restaurant. If I heard it then others have too."

"I can take care of myself," he said. "No need to worry about me, although I appreciate the warning. As to your brother's case, I can call one of the officers and ask them to work with you. That will give you access to information as well as the muscle of the police department helping you."

She shook her head. "You still don't get it, do you? Yes, if you were still the chief, it would be easier. But I don't believe any of those other cops will dig into the case the way you will."

He rolled his eyes. "Like I dug into it originally, classifying it as an accident?"

She shook her head again. "Anyone would have classified it as an accident. The only reason I doubt it is because of who the victim really was, a fact I don't want to spread around. You know he was my brother. No one else does, not the police at least. I want to keep it that way so I can stay under the radar of whoever killed him, if he really was murdered."

"Tanya Jericho's parents wouldn't agree with your faith in my investigative abilities."

"Yes, well, grief has a way of blinding people sometimes. Which is yet another reason that I need you, someone who isn't emotional about my brother. Someone who can be objective. And someone who is very good at their job. I've researched you extensively on the internet. You aren't the kind of man to give up when you see a thread to pull. In Tanya Jericho's case, there was absolutely no reason for you or anyone else to believe she was still alive. No threads. No clues to pursue. If there was, you'd have dug in your heels and gone to the ends of the earth for a resolution. The mayor and his lawyers are idiots not to realize that. Your track record of solved cases is more than enough proof."

He frowned, not sure what to make of her little speech. "Thanks. I think."

"No need to thank me. I'm not offering flattery or platitudes. Facts are facts. What *you* need to understand is that my brother wasn't alone while here in Mystic Lake. He was with friends, people who knew his true identity. If one of them or someone with them killed Esteban, they knew they were murdering the son of Michael Covington. If my father finds out my brother was murdered, he'll go on a scorched earth policy. No one will be safe from his wrath. There's no way anyone would risk that kind of vengeance unless something big is worth killing for here in your town. I honestly have no idea what that could be. But if my fears are true, other people are in danger."

"You really are worried about the safety of people you don't know, aren't you?"

She frowned. "Well of course I am. Why wouldn't I be?"

"Why not, indeed. What about this wrath you talk about? You're painting your father out to be a mob boss."

"Now you're just being a jerk, Beau."

"Keeping it real, Covington."

"I'm not blind, okay? I'm fully aware of my father's...reputation, that it's possible he might be into...less than savory things. I also know that he would do anything to protect his family, including revenge if someone hurt one of us."

"Fair enough." He stood in indecision. Everything she'd said made sense. But working with a known criminal's daughter, no matter how sexy and smart she might be, left a bad taste in his mouth.

She pressed the button to unlock the passenger door. "Are you coming or not?"

The sound of another vehicle approaching had him glancing down the road. An unfamiliar white pickup with tinted windows had just turned onto the gravel road at the bottom of the mountain.

"Come on, Beau," she encouraged him. "Think of it as an adventure. You get to rescue the damsel in distress, kill the bad guy and save the world."

He arched his brows. "Are you quoting the *Mummy* movie at me?"

"Whatever works. Did it?"

The truck coming up behind them stopped about fifty yards back, unable to pass on this particularly narrow stretch of road.

"I already know I'm going to regret this." Beau hopped into the Jeep.

Chapter Four

About halfway up the mountain, the gravel road forked off in two directions. As Sierra turned left, she could feel Beau looking at her in surprise.

"Before you tell me your house is in the other direction, I'm not lost, okay? I want to take you to my place first, show you what I've put together so far to help us get started."

"Your place."

"My rental."

"Did you know I lived on this same mountain when you rented it?"

"Does it matter?"

He sighed heavily. "I guess not. How long have you been here in town?"

"Since mid-May."

"You've been here two months? I haven't seen you on these roads or in town."

"That's because I didn't want you to. I've followed you a few times. Okay, more than a few."

"I don't think so. I'd have noticed if the same car was tailing me repeatedly."

"Which is why I trade out my rental car every week or so." She stopped at another fork in the road, checked for oncoming traffic—which was exceedingly rare on these little mountain roads—and turned left again.

"There's no way this is a rental car," he said. "No offense, but it's seen better days. Car rental agencies only rent out new or nearly new vehicles."

"You're right. I stole this one."

She could practically feel his stare burning a hole in the side of her head. When she glanced at him, he narrowed his eyes.

"Wherever you stole it from, we're taking it back. Right now."

She started laughing. "Calm down, Chief. I was kidding. It really is a rental. Check the glove box."

He popped it open and pulled out the paperwork.

She turned right and accelerated up the steep driveway, pulling into a carport at the top beside her château.

Beau shoved the papers back into the glovebox. "Rent-a-Junker? I've never heard of a company like that. Who would want to rent a beat-up old car?"

"People who want to blend in. Like me. Besides, it's only a junker on the outside. The engine purrs like a kitten." She shut it off and popped open her door. "Welcome to my little mountain getaway."

He got out and stood beside her. "Remind me later to talk to you about how to blend in. Because this mansion…isn't it."

She cocked her head, studying the two-story stone and log facade. "I agree it's bigger than your place—"

"You could put four of my homes inside that. Maybe more."

"I wanted to be comfortable. Besides, you can't see it from the road. It's completely private and hidden. I'll bet not a single person in town even realizes anyone's living up here."

He gave her a sideways look as they started across the gravel toward the front door. "You haven't spent much time in small towns, have you?"

"No. Why?"

"I guarantee people know you're here. You're probably the talk of the town and don't even realize it."

She frowned at him as she stopped at the door. "If that was true, you'd have known I was here. When I showed up at your home, you were definitely surprised."

"Only because I've been avoiding town since before you arrived. Otherwise I'd have been plugged into the local gossip and would know all about the pretty Spanish lady renting the old Haversham place. It's been vacant a long time. No one can afford the rent except, apparently, you."

She punched a code into the electronic keypad, and the lock clicked. "We're not going to get along at all if you refer to me as Spanish. I came from Cuba, not Spain."

"But you speak Spanish."

She put her hands on her hips, tossing her hair over her shoulders. "It's not at all the same."

"Noted. My apologies."

She wasn't sure if he was teasing or not. "I'll give you a tour of the place later. Right now I want to show you the office." She led him down the marble steps into the soaring two-story family room to the far side where a set of double doors stood open.

Excited to show him what she'd done, she headed inside and stopped in the middle of the room, turning around to see his reaction.

"What the—" He let out a low whistle. "This setup rivals a NASA control room. What is all of this?"

She rolled her eyes. "You're completely exaggerating." She led the way around the room, showing him the setup she'd put together. "It's just a handful of computers daisy-chained together on one server. Well, and a backup server of course. You can't be too careful. Most of what you see on all of these tables are monitors, three per computer. It's not all that sophisticated. But it was the best I could do in a hokey little town like this. I had to make half a dozen trips to Chattanooga to get the equipment. Can you believe this place didn't have even one computer in it when I rented it? Ridiculous. How do you people survive in such low-tech conditions?"

His silence had her looking at him to see if something was wrong. He was staring at her from a few feet away, shaking his head.

"What?" she asked.

"You brought in all of this equipment?"

"Um, yeah. How else would I get it here?"

"And you connected it together, that *daisy-chain* thing you mentioned?"

"Again, yes. Why?"

"I'm not sure what I expected of a mobster's daughter, but this wasn't it. What are you, some kind of computer genius?"

"No one's ever called me a *genius*, so the answer is no. But I get by. I like technology and the advantages it provides. And I'm fortunate enough to be able to afford it, so why not utilize it?"

"Why not? Right. Aside from being beautiful and a technology guru, what else do I need to know about you?"

She crossed her arms, struggling to ignore the frisson of pleasure from his compliment. "Probably that I hate labels. Stop calling my father a *mobster*. Does he circumvent laws that make doing business far too difficult? Maybe. But he's not a drug dealer or a human trafficker. He doesn't go around shooting people or bribing officials. He's a businessman. He pays his taxes, gives millions to charities and does tremendous good in his community to take care of those in need."

He stared at her as if he thought she'd lost her mind. "Do you honestly believe all that?"

"The FBI's been after him for years, hounding him, raiding my father's homes, all in the name of justice. And what do they have to show for it? A big fat zero. He's never been arrested, not once. Don't you think if he was as horrible as they believe him to be that they'd have been able to make some charges stick at some point? It's not for lack of trying."

"Remind me to share the files I've seen about your father someday, if I'm ever able to access those files again."

She rolled her eyes. "All lies I'm sure, made up by the FBI."

"If your father is so wonderful, then why not ask him for help finding out what may or may not have actually happened to your brother?"

"I need someone cool-headed to help me, not my father."

"The law-abiding, misunderstood dad? That one?"

She stomped her foot in frustration and railed at him in a flood of Spanish.

When she stopped to catch her breath, he grinned. "You spoke too fast for me to catch all of that, but I'm pretty sure you called me a host of nasty names and questioned my legitimacy."

"At least you caught the important parts." She whirled around to head into the kitchen for a cold bottle of water when he suddenly grabbed her hand, stopping her.

"What?" she demanded, ready to rant at him again, this time in English to make sure he understood every insult.

"Those monitors over there. Is that a live shot from security cameras out front?"

"Yes, they're—wait, who is that?"

"Good question." He watched the white pickup that they'd seen earlier stop halfway up the driveway, as if the driver was debating his next move.

"We should have gone to my house first to get one of my pistols. I had to turn in my police firearm."

"No worries." She crossed to one of the desks in the enormous room and pulled open the middle drawer. "Is a .357 Magnum okay? I have others."

He took it and checked the loading. "Was this purchased legally?"

"Beggars can't be choosers."

He shook his head. "Wait here. Lock the door behind me."

He jogged across the family room with her hurrying to catch up. Then he was out the door and disappeared behind some bushes.

Chapter Five

Beau crouched behind a thick shrub and peered through the branches at the white pickup. It appeared to be empty. But the window tint was so dark, it was hard to tell. Definitely darker than the legal limit. If he was still wearing a badge, he'd write the driver up for that.

After he found him.

He scanned the trees and other shrubs that blocked far too much of his view. What was it with people? Didn't they realize that planting vegetation so thick near their homes was a safety hazard? They could walk out the front door right on top of a bear without even seeing it or, worse, some thug with a gun bent on causing them harm.

Like the one creeping around the Jeep in the carport, looking in the windows right this minute. Except that it wasn't a thug.

It was Officer Collier.

Beau shook his head and pocketed the huge pistol that he had no intention of returning to Sierra until he was certain it was legal. He walked up behind his former officer—as of less than an hour ago—and tapped him on the shoulder.

Collier whirled around, scrabbling for his weapon.

Beau grabbed it and jerked it away from him. "Good grief, you're slow. I could have shot you dead before you even got it out of your holster."

"Well, I wasn't expecting someone to sneak up on me. I was just trying to see whether I was at the right house, that this was the vehicle I saw earlier, when I noticed you inside."

"And now you know it was. Why are you sneaking around up here in a truck that I know darn well isn't yours? What do you want, Collier? I told you not to try to get me to go back. And I'm sure as hell not going to beg the mayor to rehire me. I'm done." Beau handed him back his gun.

Collier holstered it. "I borrowed a vehicle I impounded yesterday from one of the town's resident drunks. I didn't want you to recognize me when I followed you."

Beau swore.

"And what I want," Collier continued, "the first thing at least, is for you to call me Chris. We're no longer boss and employee. It would be nice not to be called by my last name anymore."

"That's why you came here? To complain that I should be less formal?"

"No, but you gave me an opening. So I took it. Beau."

"Don't press your luck. Collier."

Collier cleared his throat. "Right. Not ready for first names. Okay, Chief. I mean, um—"

"Dawson works. What do you want?"

"If you're absolutely positive you're not going to be the chief anymore, my coming here is a moot point. But I was going to tell you that as soon as I got back in the station they held the vote. Want to know the result?"

"The result doesn't matter."

Collier crossed his arms. "You're not the least bit curious?"

Beau was about to lie, but he sighed instead. "I'll probably regret asking. What was the vote?"

"Us officers didn't get to cast a ballot. And the voting was anonymous—just folded slips of paper in a cup. Then the mayor's assistant counted them out. Boss, it was twelve to one in favor of keeping you on as the chief. And we both know who the one was."

"The mayor."

"Yep. It's all about the money to him, specifically the Jericho family's lawsuit, not what's right or wrong. Anyway, there's no reason for you to worry about begging the mayor for your job back. Just rescind your resignation. The town council will support you a hundred percent. Heck, after this little coup attempt the mayor will be lucky if he doesn't get thrown out of office."

"I'm not coming back."

Collier's smile faded. "I don't understand. You love being chief. And you're good at it. Obviously everyone who matters—everyone besides the mayor—agrees."

"Not the Jerichos. And not Tanya, either, I'd guess. Since she's a minor, she's not officially part of her parents' lawsuit. But I can't imagine them stirring all of this up if she wasn't okay with it."

"They're acting based on emotion. They don't understand how investigations work, how we have to follow the evidence, and if there isn't any, we're at a dead end. It's not your fault that—"

"It is my fault, Collier. I'm the one who put an end to the search for Tanya. If I hadn't, if I'd pushed a little harder, we might have gotten one more tip, one more lead that would have helped us find her. The case went cold, and we moved on based on my decision."

"There's not a law enforcement person in this county who could legitimately fault the decision you made. We spent months trying to find her. The mayor himself pressured you to stop long before we did even though he seems to have forgotten that. I specifically remember him saying you were wasting resources. If anyone should be fired or quit, it's him. Come back, Chief. We need you. Not that inexperienced joke the mayor's talking about potentially hiring."

"He's already got a replacement lined up?"

Collier sighed. "He declared me as acting chief, for now. But he said he wants the new official chief to be someone who knows our procedures already, someone who can step right into the job and keep things going smoothly." He pressed a hand to his heart, as if in physical pain. "He's planning to track down and offer the job to that narcissistic loser, Kevin Sumner."

Beau stared at him in surprise, wondering if he could have possibly heard him correctly. "Sumner? The officer who worked for us two years ago for a whole three months before I fired him for incompetence? That Kevin Sumner?"

"One and the same. Apparently some tiny department a few counties over, an even smaller department than ours, was desperate for warm bodies to fill their seats and hired him. I can't imagine they aren't regretting that decision. He's likely been put on notice and is on a mandatory improvement plan, one step away from being fired just like what happened here. If the town council approves the offer, the mayor will extend it. And we both know Sumner will jump at the chance to boss around everyone who used to tell him what to do. You have to come back. I can't work for that idiot. I'll either be fired for insubordination or will come under suspicion after Sumner goes mysteriously missing."

Beau leaned back against the Jeep. "I'm sorry. I truly am. But I can't go back. Not now. I've already got another job."

Collier's eyes widened in shock. "That's impossible. You just resigned an hour ago, if that. Wait. Is that what you've been doing during your administrative leave? Interviewing for other jobs? You planned all along to ditch us?"

The hurt in his former officer's eyes had Beau regretting even telling him. "Not at all. I spent my time reexamining my life, considering what I wanted to do going forward. Even if there hadn't been a vote, I'd likely have quit. If nothing else, my resignation helps the Jerichos feel better. And I'm not fit for duty right now, regardless. I'm not the confident man I was before everything happened with Tanya and the Phantom. I doubt myself every damn day, every decision I make. That's not the kind of man who should be leading others."

Collier leaned against the Jeep beside him. "When you say it that way, I get it. But that doesn't mean you need to permanently quit. Extend your leave. Go see a shrink or get drunk or whatever you need to do to work through this. You're too damn good to quit, boss."

They stayed there a few minutes in silence, looking out at the trees around them.

Finally, Collier straightened. "Are you going to tell me about this job? The one you supposedly weren't looking for while on leave?"

"I'm not lying about that. It's a recent development."

"How recent?"

"This morning. Right before I learned about the secret meeting to vote me out."

"And that stupid meeting helped you make the decision to resign?"

"Sometimes timing is everything. Speaking of that new job, I need to get to work right now. And you need to get back to your work before the mayor paints a target on your back too."

"Where is this job? Here? At the Haversham mansion? I heard some Spanish lady rented it."

"Cuban. Or so she tells me. It's not a formal job or anything like that. I'm just helping her, doing a favor. Kind of investigating on the side."

"Going into the private sector. I hear there's a lot more money in that. Maybe I should help you."

"No thank you." The feminine voice had both of them turning to see Sierra standing about ten feet away.

The tension on her face told Beau something was wrong.

"What is it?" he asked.

She was holding her phone and started toward him, then stopped, looking at Collier. "Do you trust him?"

Collier narrowed his eyes.

Beau held up his hands. "Truce, all right? Collier, forget you ever saw this woman. I can't introduce you two. And her safety depends on no one knowing she's here."

"We don't have time for this, Beau." She hurried to him and held up her phone. "Get mad at me later, but I planted a minicamera inside your foyer to make sure I could keep an eye on you, to make sure you were safe."

"What the—"

"This just happened. Look." She turned the phone to face him. Collier edged up beside him to watch the video she played.

The front door of Beau's cabin burst open, splintered wood from the ruined frame flying around the foyer as the door slammed back against the wall. Four men dressed in black wearing ski masks rushed inside. They split up, running past the camera.

"Who the hell are they?" Collier demanded.

Sierra gave Beau a sharp look. "I told you that you could be in danger."

"Can't fault you there," he said.

Collier looked back and forth between them. "The chief's in danger?"

"Sorry, Beau," she said. "I thought we had more time."

"Okay," Collier said. "While you two carry on your little insider conversation without me, I'll call for backup." He pulled out his phone.

Beau took it from him and shook his head. "This one isn't for the police. Not yet, anyway. This is the job I was telling you about. Go home, Collier. Or back to the station. Just pretend you didn't see that video. I've got this."

"Four ninjas just busted into your house!"

Beau rolled his eyes.

"You're not taking care of this alone," Collier said. "*We've* got this. And you can't tell me otherwise. You're not my boss anymore, remember? Besides, that impounded truck I borrowed is blocking the driveway. We go together or you don't go at all."

Collier ran to where he'd parked and hopped in the driver's seat. "You coming or not?" he yelled out the window.

Beau ran after him. As soon as he hopped in the passenger seat and slammed the door shut, the truck bounced up and down. He looked at Collier, then they both turned and looked over their shoulders.

Sierra was in the truck bed, holding a sawed-off shotgun.

Definitely *not* legal. Where the heck had she gotten it from to have grabbed it so quickly? Did she hide guns all over the yard, under the bushes? Maybe that was the kind of training the daughter of a crime boss received while other daughters were getting their nails done and going shopping.

"Get out," Beau yelled through the window.

"I can either ride with you or I'll follow in my Jeep," she yelled back.

Collier laughed. "She's got a point."

"Aw, hell. Just go."

Collier shoved the truck in Reverse.

Chapter Six

Beau braced his hands on the truck's dash as it skidded to a halt on the gravel road in front of his driveway.

"Are you *trying* to throw her out of the truck bed?" he demanded.

"Sorry. Guess I was going a little too fast."

"No kidding."

They both turned to check on Sierra. The truck bed was empty. Panic had Beau throwing open the door and jumping out to scan the road, worried he'd see her crumpled body because of Collier's deplorable driving skills.

He saw her body, all right. But she hadn't fallen out of the truck. She was jogging into the trees, her sawed-off shotgun slung over her shoulder.

"What the— Sierra, get back here." He took off after her, not waiting for Collier.

For such a small woman, she sure was fast and surprisingly quiet as she made her way toward his cabin. He didn't catch up to her until she was about to step into the clearing in front of the porch, not far from his massive woodpile.

He clapped a hand over her mouth and jerked her back into the cover of trees before anyone in the house might see her.

She bit him.

He jerked his hand back. "You little— I can't believe you did that." He turned his hand back and forth looking at it.

"I didn't break the skin. You'll survive. Don't ever put your hand over my mouth and manhandle me again. I won't stand for it."

He flexed his bruised hand. "Noted. Never mind that I was trying to save your life."

"I've got a pretty significant weapon on me capable of inflicting major damage. I can take care of myself. And we're wasting time hiding in the bushes." She ran around him and entered the clearing.

"Sierra, stop," he called out.

Bam! Bam! Bullets strafed the dirt inches from her feet.

Beau grabbed her around the waist and whirled around, firing the .357 Magnum toward his house to cover them as he yanked her behind a tree.

Collier dropped to a knee beside them. "Where did those shots come from?"

"The far right corner. My bedroom. The window's open. One of them must have seen Genius here when she offered herself up for target practice."

She glared at him and slapped at his hands until he let her go. "If you hadn't stopped me, I might have been able to take him out."

"Did you know what direction he was shooting from so you could fire back?"

Her lips pursed.

"I didn't think so. And you're welcome."

"When I get over being mad at you, I'll thank you."

"Don't do me any favors."

She frowned. "Any element of surprise we had is gone. What do we do now?"

Collier held up his phone, then shoved it in his pocket. "Already done. I just called for backup. And don't tell me I shouldn't have, Chief. This isn't a simple smash-and-grab. If they were here to rob the place they'd have been out by now and they wouldn't be trying to kill us. Any idea who these guys might be and what they want? Sierra, earlier you mentioned danger to the chief. What's that about?"

"It's Dawson," Beau corrected him.

"What?"

"I'm not the chief anymore."

"Oh, good grief," Collier griped.

"Um, guys?" Sierra held up her phone, showing them the view from the camera she'd put in the foyer. "There are two men with rifles in the front of the house. They just passed the camera and took up positions by the front windows."

"Rifles?" Beau and Collier both asked.

"Well, they didn't look like shotguns so I think so. Why?"

They swore.

Beau grabbed her again, this time tossing her over his shoulder in spite of her shriek of outrage. He took off running toward the road with Collier running full out beside him.

The sound of glass shattering was their only warning. Sharp cracks of rifle fire sounded and bullets began pinging off trees, sending sharp bits of wood flying at them.

"Ouch," Collier brushed wood from his hair.

"Go, go, go," Beau yelled. "We're seriously outgunned."

"I've got a shotgun, for crying out loud," Sierra called out, each word punctuated with a grunt as she bounced on his shoulder.

"Far enough?" Collier yelled.

"Far enough." Beau slid to a halt in the dirt and set Sierra down.

He was fast becoming familiar with her glare as she aimed it at him again. She jerked her shotgun off her shoulder and held it up. "Why are we running from these guys when I've got this? We should circle back and—"

"Get yourself killed?" Beau snatched the gun from her. "A shotgun doesn't have the range that a rifle has. Neither do our pistols. We need a plan. What's the ETA on backup, Collier?"

He worked his mouth, a red flush creeping up his neck. "Um, it might be a bit. After the meeting the mayor was so angry he sent everyone home. It'll take a while to get them up here."

"Understood," Beau said.

Sierra glanced back and forth between them. "I don't understand at all. Everyone left? Who's in charge at the police station?"

"As acting chief, I treated it like end of shift," Collier said.

"End of shift? What does that even mean?"

Beau glanced at Collier before answering her. "Mystic Lake has a relatively low crime rate and a staff of only four police officers in addition to the police chief. When the day shift ends, or if there's a situation where all of the officers are needed elsewhere, the station is locked up and the department's phones go to a switchboard in Chattanooga. Only 911 emergencies get routed to a Mystic Lake police officer's cell phone. Everything else is tabled until morning."

"Who the heck set that kind of policy?" she demanded.

Beau cleared his throat. "I did. We went four years without a single call at night and then we were short of needed officers during the day shift because of staffing the station twenty-four seven all the time. I decided to move everyone to the day shift and instituted a partnership with the Chattanooga sheriff's office for phone coverage after hours. Like I said, there are only four regular officers. Do the math."

"Now I understand my brother being killed. He could have been chased or stalked or whatever and never had a chance in a town with no law enforcement to speak of."

Beau gave her an incredulous look. "I couldn't convince you to go to the station this morning. And now you expect me to believe your brother would have called the police if he thought someone was after him?"

Her face flushed. "He might have, if he was in trouble and had no other option."

"Wait," Collier said. "Your brother's name is Esteban? And you're Sierra?" His eyes widened. "No way. You're a Covington?"

She blew out a disgusted breath. "Give me back my shotgun. Now I have to kill him."

Collier took a quick step back.

"She's kidding." Beau gave her a sideways glance. "I think."

She crossed her arms, remaining silent.

"What's the plan, Acting-Chief Collier?" Beau leaned back against one of the trees.

"Uh…well, I suppose we don't have much choice. We should retreat, return to my truck and head down the road a bit, stay out of sight until reinforcements arrive."

"Definitely an option," Beau agreed. "Probably the safest one."

"For cowards," Sierra complained.

"You have a better plan?" Beau asked.

"We tried a frontal assault. Or, at least, we would have if you hadn't interfered. What's the situation at the back of your cabin? Any way we could circle around and surprise them?"

Collier chuckled. "If you have some mountain climbing equipment. The back of his house is on stilts, sunk into the bedrock. It's a fifty foot drop off his deck, straight down."

"We can't cower here and wait on the police," she said. "By the time they get here, those guys might sneak off in the woods and will be long gone. We need to catch them and find out who they are."

Collier looked from one to the other. "Why? What's really going on here that, one, there are apparently cameras inside the chief's cabin and, two, you both seem to want to catch these guys? And don't tell me it's all about justice. What's this really about?"

"You're right," Beau said.

"I am? Right about what?"

"Not you, Collier. Sierra. We can't wait here and let them get away. Either of you notice anything? Like how quiet it is now?"

Sierra's eyes widened. "They're not shooting anymore." She grabbed her phone and checked her app, running through the more recent video in addition to the live feed. "They headed back through the foyer about five minutes ago. All of them. Four guys."

"Show me." Beau scooted closer and watched her run through the video. "Stop. Back up. There. See that?"

She studied the screen, zooming in on the frame. "*Caramba*. They're getting away."

Beau grabbed her hands and pulled her to her feet. He passed her the shotgun and took out his pistol.

"Uh, guys. What's going on?" Collier pulled out his gun.

Beau and Sierra took off running through the woods toward the cabin. Collier called out and hurried after them.

They all stopped at the tree line, right where they'd started. The silence from the house was almost as eerie as the earlier gunfire.

"Police, freeze!" Beau yelled.

Collier gave him a sideways glance. "That's my line."

"Habit."

Collier laughed. "Mystic Lake Police Department. You're surrounded. Drop your weapons. Come out with your hands up."

"They're surrounded? Really?" Beau arched a brow.

"They don't know that they're not."

Beau laughed, then grabbed a rock and tossed it at the front porch. It landed with a loud thud.

Silence.

Sierra checked her phone. "Nothing. I think they're gone."

"Gone where?" Collier asked. "What did you see in the video?"

"Just a glimpse of the sliders from the foyer," Beau said. "The ones off the back deck that you said wasn't scalable. They all headed out but never came back inside."

"Did they have ropes with them?" Collier asked.

"Not that I saw." Beau gripped his pistol tighter. "You should both stay here, in case this is a trick and they're waiting to ambush whoever comes through that door. It's not like one little camera is going to catch everything they do." He turned to look at Collier. "You okay with that plan?"

"Um, sure, Chief. But I don't think Sierra agrees." He pointed toward the house.

Beau whirled around to see her sprinting toward the porch, shotgun out in front of her.

He bolted after her, catching up just as she flung the front door open. He grabbed her and jerked her to the side as he ducked down and aimed his pistol inside.

She flung his arm off her, swearing at him in a mixture of English and Spanish.

He couldn't help grinning. "Your accent gets really noticeable when you're angry."

Her eyes narrowed, but before she could say anything, Collier jogged up beside Beau, aiming his gun inside the foyer.

"Clear." He slid in past them and swung his gun toward the right side, the kitchen area. "Clear."

Beau rushed into the foyer, covering him from his left side. "Clear." He motioned toward the back doors on either side of the fireplace, indicating Collier should go right while he went left. He held up his fingers, counting down from three. Two. One.

They rushed into the living area, diving and rolling past the sliders and coming up on opposite ends of the large room, guns aimed out at the deck.

Beau leaned forward, peering through the glass, looking left and right. He glanced over at Collier who looked at him and shook his head. Nothing. No sign of the intruders on the deck.

Remaining silent, they cleared all the rooms down the long hall, quickly and efficiently as a well-oiled team used to training and working together for years. The house was definitely empty. Now to see where the men had gone.

Heading up the hallway toward the living room, Beau said, "Let's head out onto the deck. They must have had some equipment out there already and rappelled down. There's no other exit. Let's go."

They emerged from the hall and Beau started swearing again. The slider on the right side was open and Sierra was stepping into the family room from the deck.

"Clear," she said, mimicking them. "No sign of the ninjas."

"I really wish you would stop charging off on your own like that," Beau told her. "It's dangerous." He moved past her along with Collier, and they aimed their guns over the railing.

Beau stopped at the far left side, then shook his head and shoved his pistol in his holster. "I should have thought of that."

Collier strode to him and looked down. "What is that thing?"

Sierra pushed her way in between them to see what they were looking at. "That large wooden box against the back corner of the house?"

"It's not a box," Beau said. "It's a lean-to, more or less, covering a compost barrel. I never come to the back of the house down there, forgot it was even there. It came with the house, but I'm not into composting. You can see the deep footprints beside it, right at the house's foundation."

"They jumped," Collier said. "And ran off into the woods on that side of the cabin. Gutsy."

"Reckless and stupid," Beau said. "If they hadn't landed just right they'd have pitched over the side of the mountain." He met Sierra's troubled dark brown gaze. "I'm guessing they were worried about all the noise they'd made and whether someone, if not us, would call the police."

"Speaking of police," Collier said, "sounds like a couple of ours are on the way up the mountain."

Sure enough, muted sirens sounded in the distance, signaling the impending arrival of one or more of Beau's former employees.

"I can't be seen by the cops." Sierra hurried into the family room.

"Um, hello. I'm a police officer and have already seen you," Collier called out behind Beau as they followed her inside. "Have you done something illegal I need to know about? I mean, other than being a Covington, of course."

She glared at him. "Being a Covington doesn't mean I'm a criminal."

"The sawed-off shotgun kind of ruins your point," Beau said drily.

"I should take that." Collier reached for it, and she jerked it away, bringing it up toward him instead.

Beau yanked it out of her hand. "Point that at him or any

of my officers again and this alleged partnership you want is over before it really begins. Hell, I'll be the one to haul you to jail, regardless of my current law enforcement status."

Her chin tilted up in defiance. But she didn't try to grab the gun again.

Beau handed it to Collier.

She put her hands on her hips. "I need that. Those guys are getting away. I need to catch up to them, see them without their masks so I know who I'm dealing with. They could be the ones behind my brother's death. I can't go unarmed. I need protection."

"I'm your protection," Beau practically growled. "We do this my way or not at all."

"Who made you the boss?" she demanded.

"You did, when you came here asking me for help."

The sirens were getting louder now, closer.

Beau glanced toward the front windows or what was left of them. "The police will be at the house soon. You want to follow the trail, Sierra. So do I. But we do it together, as a team, or we stay here and you get to explain why you're in Mystic Lake with an illegal firearm. Choose."

"Chief," Collier said. "You both need to stay so we can straighten this out. I'm not going to lie about what happened or cover up who she is."

"That's it. Give me my gun." Sierra narrowed her eyes.

Beau arched a brow. "Collier, do what you have to do."

Collier expertly snapped a handcuff on her wrist then swung her around to cuff the other one before she realized what was happening.

"What are you doing?" She twisted and jerked her arms, trying to pull her wrists out of the cuffs. "I haven't done anything wrong. Beau. Help me. Wait, where are you going?"

"Chief?" Collier echoed. "Don't. Please."

Beau stopped at the front door. “I have bad guys to catch.” He ignored both of their pleas as he ran out of the cabin and sprinted off in the direction where the gunmen had disappeared.

Chapter Seven

It had been at least half an hour since the four gunmen had fled Beau's home. They'd had an excellent head start and should have been long gone by the time he tracked them through the woods. And yet, here they were, about thirty feet away, lounging around as if they had all the time in the world. What were they up to? And what were they waiting for?

Careful to be as quiet as possible and avoid stepping on twigs or anything else that might make a sound and alert them to his presence, Beau edged closer. At twenty feet away, he was as close as he dared, concealed within a thick group of bushes. As long as he didn't move or make a noise, they shouldn't see him even if they walked right past him. Or so he hoped.

Confronting them, unfortunately, wasn't an option. Not only was he outgunned, these henchmen were spread around the clearing rather than sitting together. If he did end up having to fire at them, they'd see his muzzle flash and be able to aim right at him before he could take all of them out.

Not that he wanted to do that.

Losing his job didn't mean he'd lost his ethics, his morals, his sense of right and wrong. The law mattered. Justice mattered. His goal wasn't to kill them. His goal was to get information, find out why they'd broken into his home armed like an elite special forces team. Although he was fairly certain it was because of what Sierra had already said about him investigating her brother's death. Them showing up after her warning was too much of a coincidence not to be related. What Beau really needed to do was identify these men so he could figure out exactly who he was up against.

But he couldn't do that by confronting them, not without backup, which wasn't even a thing for him anymore. He was a civilian now. Powerless to arrest them, even if he hadn't been outgunned. But he wasn't powerless to gather evidence with the only weapon he could safely use right now.

His phone's camera.

Carefully shielding the screen behind the bushes so no one would notice the light, he set it to silent and dimmed the screen. Then he began snapping pictures.

All four of them were dressed in black with bullet-resistant vests strapped over their shirts. Two of them had long guns hanging from straps over their shoulders. All four wore knives in scabbards at their waists. But where they'd been wearing ski masks at his cabin, here in the clearing they'd tugged them off. Because of that mistake, Beau was able to get excellent photos of their faces.

Three of them anyway.

The fourth one had his back to Beau. After taking pictures of the others, Beau kept his phone camera at the ready, waiting for the last guy to look over his shoulder or move to where Beau could snap a photo of his face.

A low buzzing sound had all of them looking toward Bad Guy Number Four, the one with his back to Beau. He tilted his head down, probably reading a text on his phone. Then he stood.

"We've finally been given an alternate pickup location, clear of cops. Head due north. Let's go."

They took off, jogging out of the clearing and heading away from Beau. He waited as long as he dared, not wanting them to hear him. Then he took off in pursuit, circling the clearing and keeping low and behind cover as much as possible. All the while, he tried picturing a map of the mountain in his head, following the twists and turns they were taking. But if they were searching for a road, they were going the wrong way. There was only one up and down this mountain. Just like there was only one road into Mystic Lake, a narrow hour-long drive through the heavy woods with tight turns. There was no other way to reach this landlocked town, except by helicopter. So what did the fourth man mean by an alternate pickup location? Even if they had a chopper, there wasn't anywhere near this particular mountain where one could safely land. The trees were too close together, the brush far too thick.

A few minutes later, the distant sound of engines gave Beau the answer. The bad guys didn't need a road. They were getting picked up by all-terrain vehicles. And if Beau didn't catch up, fast, he'd miss that pickup and his opportunity to take pictures of anyone else involved in...whatever this was. He took off at a sprint, gun out, just in case the noise he was now making was heard by any of the gunmen over the sound of the ATVs.

His lungs were burning and his legs aching by the time he caught up to them. Three of the gunmen were already wearing helmets, riding behind the drivers of the ATVs, zipping away through the woods. The last gunman, the man Beau hadn't been able to photograph earlier, remained. His posture was stiff, tense, as he stood again with his back to Beau. Across from him was the driver of the last ATV. He too was dressed all in black. But the only weapon on him was a pistol holstered at his waist. When he dismounted, he didn't bother to remove his helmet. Instead, he stalked forward in quick, angry strides.

Beau snapped pictures as best he could with the sparse cover available in this section of the woods. When the driver reached the other man, he slammed his fist into the man's jaw, knocking him to the ground.

A flurry of angry Spanish followed as the driver berated the man he'd punched. Beau's understanding of the language wasn't good enough to catch most of the words. But he did catch one that didn't require translation.

Sierra.

The driver flipped the visor of his helmet up to continue his tirade. Beau zoomed in with his camera to snap a picture, then froze, shocked. He recognized him.

The man grabbed the other guy by the arm and jerked him to standing. They jogged to the ATV and hopped on, the second man donning the extra helmet. Beau belatedly realized he'd missed his opportunity to get a picture of the fourth gunman's face. But at least he'd seen him. He could identify him if he ever saw him again. The ATV revved and the two men quickly sped away.

Beau thumbed through the last series of photos he'd taken, then stopped as the familiar face of the last driver stared back at him from his phone. He wasn't mistaken. He knew this man or, at least, knew who he was.

He closed the photo app and pressed one of the contacts in his Favorites list before beginning the long jog back toward his cabin.

The line clicked. "Chief, what are you—"

"Collier, where's Sierra?"

"Where are *you*? Did you find the gunmen? Do you need—"

"Where is she, Collier?"

"About twenty feet away glaring at me through the bars of the holding cell. We left just as the others were turning onto your street. I called and instructed them to work on evidence collection. They should still be there, at your place."

Beau jumped over a rotted log and ducked to avoid a low-hanging branch. "Did they see Sierra when you passed them?"

"Doubtful. The tint on that truck is too dark, yet another ticket I'll have to write for the owner. That tint's illegal."

"I don't care about the damn tint, Collier. Have you entered Sierra's name into the system yet?"

"Are you always this grumpy after a gunfight?"

"Collier—"

"Okay, okay. It's been a hell of a day. I get it. Sierra and I only just got to the station. Typing up the arrest report wasn't my first priority. Getting her into the cell without her biting off my arm or kicking the hell out of me was. No telling what she'd have done if she hadn't been handcuffed. I swear the woman's half-feral."

Loud swearing told Beau that Sierra didn't appreciate that comment.

"Did you tell any other officers about her?"

"Not yet. When they get here, we'll spill our guts in the conference room and decide our next steps."

"Do me a favor, Collier. Don't. Don't tell the others about Sierra. Don't put anything about her in your report. I don't want any online trace of her being there."

"Please tell me you're kidding. She brandished a shotgun at me. Heck, you told me to arrest her."

Beau dodged another low-hanging branch. "I'll explain when I get there. I'm heading toward my cabin now to get my truck and a few other things before coming to the station."

"Okay, okay. I'll wait. But if you honestly expect me not to put everything in the report and hide the truth from my fellow officers, you'll have to give me a damn good reason."

"Sierra's life could very well depend on it."

Collier let out a long-suffering sigh. "Guess I can't argue with that."

"One more thing. Keep an eye out for any strangers near the station. These are some very, very bad guys."

"No kidding. I was in the gunfight with you earlier. Remember?"

"I mean it, Collier. Be extra vigilant. Something strange is going on. Something dangerous. And Sierra is right in the middle of it."

Chapter Eight

The sound of the front door opening had Sierra sitting up straighter on the cot in the cell. Beau Dawson strode into view, his black boots creating a dull thud against the hardwood floor as he headed toward Officer Collier.

He didn't even spare her a glance as he sat beside Collier's desk, turning his chair to face the glass entry door and windows fronting Main Street.

She crossed her arms and watched the two men conversing in low tones, obviously not wanting her to hear whatever they were saying. Some of her frustration and anger at being locked up faded as she noted the tension in Beau's posture. His handsome brow was drawn into lines of worry. And his frequent glances toward the door and large plate-glass windows did even more to broadcast his concern.

It seemed safe to assume that the men who'd shot up his cabin had gotten away or they'd have been brought here in handcuffs, just like her. Was that why Beau was so worried? Did he think the gunmen would be bold enough to actually come to the station?

Collier nodded in agreement with whatever Beau had just said. Then Beau stood and crossed to what had been his office until a handful of hours ago and disappeared inside. When he came back out a few minutes later, he was wearing a black backpack. He didn't stop at Collier's desk. Instead, he crossed straight to her cell.

His dark eyes were intent, his expression a mixture of worry and determination as he punched a code into the electronic keypad on the wall. A buzzing noise sounded followed by a loud click. Then he slid open the door and motioned for her to come out.

She didn't hesitate, grateful to be free of her cage. "I was beginning to think I'd never get out of there. Your officer didn't even give me a phone call to start the bond process."

"He's no longer my officer. And he kept you here for your protection. We're leaving."

She blinked. "Where are we going? To the courthouse?"

"Mystic Lake doesn't have a courthouse."

"Right. Too small. Chattanooga, then? If you'll let me have that phone call, I can have a lawyer waiting there when we arrive. He'll bond me out so I don't get locked up again."

He arched a brow. "You seem to know a lot about the legal process. Is that from personal experience?"

She put her hands on her hips. "Not the kind you're thinking. I have, uh, friends who've been in a bit of trouble here and there."

"Friends. Right. We'll go with that. Officer Collier has graciously agreed to release you into my custody."

The stinging comeback she was about to deliver in response to his sarcastic tone died unspoken when he mentioned her being released. When he didn't elaborate, she said, "You're the one who encouraged your officer to arrest me, and now you're circumventing the legal process to get me out? No, not get me out. *Release me into your custody*, whatever that means. Why?"

"Just a precaution until Collier and the team perform their investigation."

"A precaution?"

He glanced at the street again.

She followed his gaze, then stepped in front of him to force his attention back to her. "You actually think they'll come here looking for you?"

"Or you. Or both of us." He shrugged. "I can't imagine them being brazen enough to come here. But I'm being extra cautious."

She blinked, surprised. "You think they're after me too?"

"The shootout wasn't enough to convince you?"

"It was your cabin. They were clearly targeting you."

"Sierra, the bullets strafed the ground right where you'd been standing before I yanked you into the trees."

"I was in the way, interfering with them getting you. If they'd realized who I was, they wouldn't have shot at me."

"Because they're afraid of your father?"

"Most people are."

"Because he's a simple *businessman*?" His voice practically dripped with sarcasm.

She glared at him.

He blew out a breath, his frustration obvious. "Look, I'm just trying to make a point here. If you're right and your brother was murdered, and these men were involved—which seems likely—they've already proven they're not worried about your father's wrath. What's one more Covington to them now?"

She blinked, his words chilling her as they sank in. His conclusions seemed ridiculously obvious and logical. But she'd lived so long under the umbrella of her father's protection that it hadn't dawned on her that she too could be in mortal danger. She'd foolishly believed all this time that if someone found out she was investigating her brother's death, the worst that would happen was that they'd leave town before she could finish her investigation. But now she knew the truth.

She was in just as much danger as Beau.

His voice droned on as he continued his explanation.

"—so whatever they're after, whatever reason they had for…going after your brother, at a minimum they'll want to keep you from telling anyone about your suspicions about Esteban's death. You said you overheard in town about me reopening your brother's case. They could have just as easily heard about you being in town, or at least some Spanish lady who's been hanging around. That could have led them to suspect you were the Spanish lady. They may have been watching you all this time, figuring out what to do about your interference. Until we know for sure who these men are, the safest thing to assume is that they want to silence you just as badly as they want to silence me."

She nodded in reluctant agreement, fear making her clasp her hands to keep them from trembling.

Beau gave her an empathetic look as if realizing that his words had finally gotten through to her. He lightly squeezed her shoulder. "It's going to be okay. I wasn't trying to scare you. I just wanted to make sure you understood the situation. We need to get out of here. Now."

"And go where?" she asked. "My rental house?"

He glanced at Collier, before answering. "I don't think that's a good idea. We'll discuss our destination after we leave."

She arched a brow. "You suddenly don't trust your own officer?"

"Not telling Collier where we're going is my way of protecting him. What he doesn't know can't put him in danger."

"Back door?" Collier asked.

"Back door." Beau took one of Sierra's hands in his and tugged her across the squad room.

She was so surprised that she didn't pull away or argue. Not that she minded him holding her hand. The man wasn't exactly hard on the eyes. And she hadn't had to fake her attraction to him when she'd shamelessly flirted earlier today. But letting someone pull her around and force her to do something wasn't what she'd normally allow.

As he pulled open the back door, she half-expected a gunman to meet them there. Thankfully, the doorway was empty. No gunshots rang out from the woods across the back alley.

He scanned their surroundings. Then he pulled her out with him so Collier could close the door.

"This way," Beau said, although he didn't need to tell her that since he was already tugging her along again.

She sighed and followed his lead. For now.

When the alley curved around the last of the buildings, she was surprised to see that they were at the parking lot at the beginning of Main Street. She'd never noticed an alley entrance when parking there. The way the trees curved around the buildings back here, they concealed the alley. She imagined that was by design, most likely by the police. Smart.

"Now that we're alone you can tell me where we're going," she said as he pulled her toward a black four-wheel drive pickup that she guessed was his personal vehicle.

He pressed a key fob, unlocking the doors as he stopped by the passenger side. "Chattanooga."

She hopped up in the truck. "Chattanooga? That's an hour away, just to reach the city limits. Another half hour on top of that, at least, to get downtown if we're going to the sheriff's office. If not, downtown is where all the nicer hotels are located. Isn't there somewhere else we can stay and still be safe? Somewhere in Mystic Lake?"

"That's plan B. I prefer plan A, getting you the heck out of Dodge."

He shut the door before she could ask about plan B. Once he was in the driver's seat with his backpack on the floor behind them, he started the truck and backed out of the parking space. Soon they were on the narrow road that would wind them through the mountains for over an hour before they'd arrive at what lay on the other side: Chattanooga.

She rubbed her hands across her arms, looking at the thick, dark woods crowding in on the road from either side. She'd always loved this long, beautiful drive when she'd gone in or out of town. The glimpses of rock-strewn creeks and the occasional waterfall visible through gaps in the trees were breathtaking, as were the green valleys below when they came into view. But none of those sights gave her pleasure right now. Instead, they made her uncomfortably aware of how isolated and empty this road was at this time of day with most people at work.

"Beau?"

"Hmm?"

"If you're truly worried that the gunmen who attacked us at your house will come after us, then why are we out here all by ourselves on such an isolated road? Aren't you worried they could follow us and overtake us?"

"No one's going to catch us by surprise out here. There are live camera feeds at our police station that show the entrances to this road both from Mystic Lake and from the Chattanooga side. I had those cameras put up after some trouble we had last year. And Collier confirmed earlier that there was no one out here before we started out. If he sees anyone turn onto the road from either side and doesn't recognize them as a local, he'll let me know so we can avoid them."

"Avoid them? There aren't any exits, just turnouts for sightseers to pull off the shoulder to take pictures of the valley below and the mountains. How would we avoid them?"

"There are a few spots only the locals know about where we could hide if we have to. But that won't be necessary. In addition to those cameras to warn us, I've got a duffel bag behind my seat that I loaded up at my cabin. There's enough firepower in there to engage a small army. No one's catching me outgunned again."

The tension in her began to drain away as relief took its place. "Sounds good." She checked the time on her cell phone. "As fast as you're driving, we should be on the outskirts of Chattanooga in another half hour or so. Are we going to the sheriff's office?"

"Not unless we get desperate for help. I'd prefer to keep you off anyone's radar and out of the public eye."

"Then I'll call ahead, make some hotel reservations somewhere really nice and—"

"No. We're staying off the grid. We won't be using our real names or credit cards. No electronic trails. And we won't be staying somewhere high-profile. That's exactly where someone looking for a wealthy Covington would expect you to stay and the first place they'd look."

She grimaced at the idea of where a police chief from a small town with an even smaller budget might set them up. Staying at some bug-infested motel wasn't on her bucket list. "I hope you have some fake IDs and credit cards or a lot of cash. I'm fresh out of all of that."

"I'll manage."

She stared at him in surprise. "The chief of police has a fake ID?"

"Former chief. And any ID I have is absolutely legally obtained as a sanctioned alias to be used in an emergency. Today definitely qualifies as an emergency."

"Sanctioned? By who?"

He winked. "Me."

She was so thrown off by the unexpected wink that it took a moment for her pulse to stop racing, and for what he'd said to sink in. "This is enlightening. Former Chief Beau Dawson is a budding criminal with a ready-made alias for so-called emergencies. Is there anything else shady I should know about you?"

The sudden silence had her regretting teasing him. Her research had her confident he'd never willingly do anything illegal. He had probably set up a doing-business-as identity that allowed him to legally use an alias, much like authors used pen names. It reinforced what she already knew, that he was smart and prepared.

"Beau? What happened when you chased after the gunmen in the woods?"

He sat silent for a long time. Obviously he wasn't going to answer. She sighed and looked out her side window, watching the thick, dark forest zipping past as they barreled down the road.

"Later," he finally said. "I'll tell you what happened once we're off this road and holed up somewhere."

She wanted to argue, but his expression told her it would be pointless. "I don't like being kept in the dark. But I respect that you have your reasons. How long do you expect us to have to be holed up, as you called it? I want to go back so I can continue investigating my brother's death."

"I'd rather you didn't. Leave the investigation of your brother's death to me. A good start would be to tell me why you don't believe he drowned and think that foul play was involved."

She shrugged. "It's more of a feeling than any facts I've discovered. Esteban is strong, a really good swimmer. I can't imagine him falling overboard and not coming back up. He was also with friends. Why wouldn't they have jumped into the water to help him? I'm also surprised he even came here. I'd never heard of Mystic Lake before he…before he died and I don't know where he heard of it. I guess the final straw for me is that we buried bones, not a body. Never seeing him makes it, I don't know, hard to accept. I just want to be certain what happened. And I'm not even sure how to go about that."

"Witnesses are the key. Did you know the friends he was with at the time of his accident?"

She shook her head. "No, which is another reason I'm suspicious. I spoke to the owner of the marina in Mystic Lake, where the boat was rented. He's the one who described the friends but none of the names he gave me from his records are names I've heard of before. And when I searched for them on the internet, the names were all so common that thousands of hits came up. That was a dead end. Your turn. Why would the police, you, be so quick to rule it an accidental drowning?"

"I wouldn't say it was quick. We investigated for several weeks. My officers interviewed those friends of your brothers and their stories all matched, no red flags. Of course, my officers had no reason to doubt anyone's identities and dig deeper. That's something I'll look into as I re-investigate. I'd only just begun reviewing the case file before the Jericho lawsuit put that on hold. As for your brother being an excellent swimmer, that rarely matters in our lake. There have been many strong swimmers who go under and never resurface. Mystic Lake—the lake not the town—is the second-most deadly lake in the country, right behind Lake Lanier in Georgia, for the same reason. Both lakes were formed when water submerged an existing town. There are all kinds of hidden dangers beneath the water that can snag a swimmer's clothing or hair."

She frowned. "I hadn't heard that. I don't understand."

He glanced at her, clearly surprised. "I would have expected you'd have researched the town before coming here."

"I researched people, as best I could. Not the history of the town itself."

"Fair enough. This area used to be all mountains and valleys, no lake. A long time ago, before the current town ever existed, there was another town, an unincorporated community really, without an official name. At least, not that anyone remembers or has found in any documentation. The story is that a series of storms converged in the area and diverted a river down a mountain into the main valley. The town that was here flooded with no warning. A lot of people died. Homes, entire buildings and full-size trees were buried too. The river formed what we now call Mystic Lake, and the new town built up around it."

He glanced at her before continuing his story. "The lake is incredibly deep in parts, and there's no way all of those hazards can ever be removed. We do cleanups when we can. Remove debris whenever possible. Warnings are posted in particularly hazardous areas. And we mark the channel where boaters should stay."

His knuckles whitened on the steering wheel. "Mystic Lake is enormous, stretching for miles because that river, even though it's small, still flows down the mountains to feed it. The locals respect the lake and its history, understanding the hazards. They're careful, for the most part." He grimaced. "But even they do foolish things sometimes. The mayor's own son died in the lake years ago, in a boating accident outside the marked channel. He was only in his twenties."

"How sad. Far too young to have his life cut short."

"Agreed. The dangers become more exacerbated in the summer months, when the tourists flock to town, as you've no doubt noticed. Many ignore the warnings, go where they want. And pay a high price. Every year lives are lost, either in drownings or boating accidents. But no matter how hard we try to keep people safe, it happens over and over. Some years the deaths number in the double digits."

She stared at him in horror. "Double digits?"

"Unfortunately."

"How long have you been here?"

"My whole life. I was born here."

"And you're how old?"

The corner of his mouth tilted up. "Isn't it rude to ask someone their age?"

"Only if you're a woman. And you most definitely are not. How old are you?"

He laughed. "Older than you, but not by much."

"And how would you know my age?"

"One, I'm a police officer. Two, seriously? You're Sierra Covington. Everything about you is online, in addition to police files I have access to. Have you ever tried putting your name into a search engine to see what comes up? If you think you have any true secrets in the world of the internet, especially as a well-known public figure, you're kidding yourself."

She crossed her arms, hating that he was likely right. As much as she tried to keep a low profile, far too much about her had been put out in cyber space simply because of who her father was.

"Valid points," she conceded, "everything you've said. But I won't accept that Esteban's death was an accidental drowning unless I can confirm it somehow. Not that I was doing well in that department before I decided to reach out to you. I had the technology, the fancy equipment, but no investigative know-how. You agreed to work with me. Now you're saying you don't want me involved."

"It's not that I don't want your input. I just don't want you out and about, putting yourself in danger. Leave that to me. The investigation has to be on my terms. We return to Mystic Lake if, or when, I deem it safe. And there are some ground rules you'll have to agree to as well."

"Ground rules? Like what?"

"Non-negotiable ground rules. Rule number one. Never, ever, point a gun at one of my officers again. At any officer. Understood?"

She scoffed. "I wouldn't have actually shot him."

His expression told her he didn't believe her. "Rule number two. Don't point a gun at someone unless you're prepared to actually shoot them. Guns aren't toys. They're inherently dangerous, even in the hands of the most experienced gunman. Accidents happen. Guns go off. Which takes me back to rule number one. You agree to both of those rules, right now, or you'll never have my help with your investigation. I mean it, Sierra. Say it."

She blew out a long breath. "Fine. I agree with rule number one and rule number two. How many more rules are there?"

"I'm not sure. I'm making this up as I go."

She couldn't help but laugh. "You made up that whole plan A and plan B thing too, right? There is no plan B."

"Oh, there's definitely a plan B. But like I said, getting you safely out of this area and into hiding in Chattanooga is our best option by far." He checked the time on his phone's screen. "We'll reach the interstate in less than twenty minutes. From there it should be smooth sailing."

She looked out her passenger-side window again, glad that he was going to work on the investigation. But there were limits to what he'd do in his pursuit of the truth, lines she doubted he'd cross as a cop, or former cop.

And lines she would.

Esteban was her brother. Her oldest biological sibling. She'd do anything necessary to discover who'd killed him and why. Then she'd get justice. The problem was that her concept of justice and Beau's weren't the same. Sitting around for years to hope the legal system worked in her favor and punished those guilty of killing Esteban wasn't something she was willing to do. When the time came, she and Beau could end up on opposite sides. Enemies.

Tires screeched. The truck jerked, throwing her against her seat belt. She threw her hands up on the dash, bracing herself as the truck skidded to a stop.

She stared through the windshield in shock. No more than fifty yards ahead of them, a large dark-colored SUV sat facing them in the middle of the road. The doors were open. And behind each one stood a man holding a rifle aimed at them.

Chapter Nine

"Sweet Lord," Sierra whispered, as she unclicked her seat belt.

Beau reached behind their seats, then tossed something bulky and heavy in her lap. "Put that on. I should have had you do it at the station. I won't underestimate them again."

"I don't… I don't understand. I thought you said there were cameras, that Collier would call us—"

"There are. He would. They must have tapped into the live feeds and set them on a recorded loop so that all Collier sees on his screens is an empty road. It's the only thing that makes sense. Hurry, put that on."

She looked down at what he'd tossed to her, then swallowed hard. "Kevlar? Wait, where's yours?"

"On you. Or it will be, in a minute. Hurry. We don't have time to argue."

He reached between them again, this time coming up with a rifle. Except, not any kind of rifle she'd ever seen before. It was huge, menacing and looked as if it could rip open the side of a tank. She sent up a quick, silent prayer as she shrugged into the vest and tightened the straps.

Beau rolled down his window and settled the end of the rifle on top of the side-view mirror, aiming it at the truck blocking the road.

"Get on the floor, Sierra."

"Beau—"

"Now."

She turned around and slid into the floor, tugging at the cumbersome Kevlar vest to squeeze into the tight space. No sooner had she ducked her head down on the front of her seat than the sound of gunshots echoed around them as the gunmen let loose with a volley of shots. Beau's answering shots boomed like a cannon inside the truck. Sierra gasped and covered her ears, trying to shut out the sound.

Bullets pinged off metal. Glass exploded above her as the windshield shattered and sprinkled down on her like rain. She squeezed her eyes shut as the terrifying barrage continued.

And then, just as suddenly as it had begun, everything stopped. The silence was broken only by the sound of Beau's deep ragged breaths. And one brief, keening moan from somewhere outside.

She looked up, noting the tension carved in his face as he stared through the hole framed by the ragged edges of what remained of the windshield.

"Beau," she whispered, "what's—"

"Stay down. Wait here." He set his cell phone on her seat. "Call Collier. Tell him what's going on. He's listed in the Favorites." He popped open his door and hopped down, his boots crunching on glass as he jogged down the road.

Sierra grabbed the phone and made the call. She waited, but it didn't ring. A quick look at the screen showed no bars, no service. She tried again anyway, but when it didn't go through, she tossed the phone into the console and tried to unwedge herself from the tight space in the floor. The heavy bulletproof vest kept pulling at her as if she was swimming in quicksand, but she finally got free and plopped onto the seat.

Staying low, she peered over the top of the dash, then drew a sharp breath. The SUV blocking the road was in utter ruins. The tires were shredded. Large pieces of rubber littered the road. Every window appeared to have been shot out. Glass was everywhere. Enormous holes pockmarked the doors. One sagged down at an awkward angle from its only remaining hinge, scraping the asphalt. But the real damage was to the men who'd been standing by the SUV. Three of them lay crumpled and unmoving on the road. Blood streaked across their clothes and pooled beneath them. But one man must have still been alive. Beau was on his knees beside him, apparently checking his injuries.

Sierra's hands shook as she leaned back between the seats to see what else Beau had in his truck. Unsurprisingly, there was a large first-aid kit in the duffle bag he'd mentioned earlier. She grabbed it and hopped out.

Beau's head jerked up as she ran toward him.

"Get back in the truck," he shouted.

She ignored his latest order and used her shoe to sweep a spot relatively clear of glass before getting on her knees beside the gunman across from Beau. The man's eyes were closed, and he wasn't moving. But his chest was rising and falling. He was breathing, but appeared to be unconscious.

"It's not safe," Beau hissed at her. "These guys could have backup on the way."

"Then, I'll have to be fast." She threw open the kit and grabbed some gauze packets, ripping them open and shoving Beau's hands away so she could take over.

He didn't try to stop her again. Instead, he yanked out his pistol and held it down by his side as he looked around.

"What did Collier say?" he asked.

"Nothing. I couldn't get the call to go through. No service."

"I've never had problems with cell service on this road."

"I couldn't get a call out. And I know how to use a phone."

"Maybe there are sunspots or something interfering with

the signal. We'll have to take him with us to get medical help."

"If I can't get this bleeding stopped he won't make it." Sierra tore open a fresh pack of gauze and pressed it down over the blood-soaked ones, applying pressure again.

"Do you have a phone on you?" Beau asked. "Maybe we have service here on the road."

"Here, press down while I get it out."

He took over while she slid her phone out of her pants pocket. Beau told her the number, and she tried it, then shook her head. "Nothing." She held her phone out. "Try yourself, if you want."

"No need. I trust you. These bandages are soaked through."

She checked the first-aid kit. "The rest are too small. We need something bigger, thicker."

"Take over." He lifted his hands, and she immediately covered the bloody gauze with her own hands, desperately trying to stanch the flow of blood that kept oozing down the man's sides.

A moment later, a wadded up shirt dropped down on top of her hands. She glanced up, expecting to see a shirtless Beau. But she quickly realized it wasn't his shirt. He was folding up a knife and putting it away next to one of the dead men, whose bullet-riddled chest was now minus a shirt. Beau had cut it off him.

She grabbed it and placed it over the bandages before pressing down again.

Beneath her, the man moaned.

"Sorry," she said. "I know this must hurt. We have to stop the bleeding."

The man didn't respond, no doubt slipping back into unconsciousness, which was probably for the better.

"What do we do now?" she asked when Beau dropped down across from her again.

"We'll have to load him into the truck and take him to Stella's B and B. She's a retired nurse. We don't have any doctors in town. But I've seen her save people against tremendous odds. Another change I made this year was to keep more emergency supplies stocked at her place. We don't have blood, but she can pump up his blood volume with an IV."

"Wouldn't it be better to take him to the hospital in Chattanooga? He definitely needs a transfusion. And we're closer to Chattanooga now than Mystic Lake."

"It's a risk either way. We're only fifteen or twenty minutes from the city limits. But it's another thirty or forty minutes after that by car to the hospital, and that's only if there's no traffic, which pretty much never happens. We're only about thirty-five minutes total from the B and B. If Stella can stabilize him, we can fly him to the hospital in the town's medevac chopper."

"The town doesn't have a doctor but you have a chopper?"

"Donation from a wealthy resident. We need to tie that shirt down tight to keep the pressure on when we move him. He's fairly thin. I can probably tie more shirts around him in a tight knot to keep that one in place. Maybe even use a belt as a tourniquet of sorts to tighten it down. Are you doing okay? Do you need me to take over?"

"I'm okay. But hurry. My arms are starting to get rubbery from pressing down so hard."

"I'll be quick."

True to his word, he was back in less than a minute with more shirts. These were, thankfully, less bloody than the first one he'd brought. But it made her wonder where those men had been shot, if not in the chest. She didn't look over to confirm her fears.

With both of them working together, they got the shirts knotted and held into place with a belt from one of the dead men.

"I think it's working," Sierra said. "There's barely a trickle now."

"Good. He can't afford to lose much more blood. He's white as a sheet."

She looked at the man's alarmingly pale face, her breath catching in her throat. "This is ridiculous. He was trying to kill us, and here we are trying to save him. I don't know why we even care." Even as she said it, she gently pressed her fingers against the side of his neck, feeling for his pulse.

"Because we're not like him," Beau said, his voice tight.

She glanced up, then looked back down. "His pulse is weak. His breathing is really shallow. He's lost far too much blood. I don't… I don't think he'll make it back to Mystic Lake or to Chattanooga. I don't know what else we can do."

Beau hesitated, then grabbed the first-aid kit and set it down beside him. He rummaged inside. "What about stitches? Do you think that would make a difference? I have needles and thread in the kit."

She shook her head. "I think your makeshift tourniquet is working just as well or better than stitches. It's blood that he needs."

"How about mine?" a raspy voice called out.

Sierra jerked her head up.

Beau grabbed his pistol and swung it toward the man stepping out of the woods. He was nearly as tall as Beau and just as muscular, dressed all in black like the men from the SUV. But his facial features were concealed behind the tinted facial shield of his motorcycle helmet.

"Hands up," Beau ordered.

The man slowly raised his hands. "I'm unarmed."

"Dressed exactly like the men who attacked my home earlier. And like all of these men who tried to kill us," Beau accused. "I'll bet your gun isn't far away."

"His name is Randy," the man said, notably not responding to Beau's comments about his clothes or a gun. "He's O positive. So am I. You can do a direct transfusion from me to him."

"Or we can transport him to town instead," Beau said.

"I heard you talking about his options, or lack of them. The woman said she doesn't think he'd make it, not without blood."

"Maybe the guy should have thought of that before he and his men opened fire on us."

The man's helmet cocked to the side, as if he was studying Beau. "If you were really that callous, you wouldn't be out in the road with…with this woman, trying to save him. You're obviously not the murderer type."

Sierra stared at the motorcycle man. He seemed familiar, but she couldn't put her finger on why.

A muscle flexed in Beau's jaw, his dark eyes flashing with anger. "Doesn't matter. We can't do a transfusion anyway. My first-aid kit doesn't have those kinds of supplies."

"Check the back of the SUV. Maybe there's a more substantial medical kit in there."

Beau narrowed his eyes. "Is that something you know firsthand?"

The man didn't answer.

"Even if we have supplies at hand, I don't have a clue how to do a transfusion."

"I've done it before," the man said. "I can talk you through it."

"No need." This time it was Sierra who spoke. "I've seen it done a couple of times." Without waiting for Beau's decision, she jumped up and jogged to the back of the SUV, ignoring his loud swearing behind her. Sure enough, when she opened the back there was a large black duffel bag. When she unzipped it, it was like looking at the inside of a hospital emergency room. "Good grief," she whispered. "These guys are prepared for a siege."

She quickly grabbed what she needed, then hurried back to the man on the ground. If anything, he looked even paler than before. And he had an alarming tinge of blue around his lips.

She motioned toward the guy in the helmet and started setting out her supplies on a sterile disposable drape she'd brought from the kit. "Hurry."

His helmet swiveled toward Beau as if waiting for permission.

Beau handed Sierra his pistol. "Keep this trained on him while I search him for weapons. One wrong move, shoot. Even if you have to go through me."

"*Madre de Dios*," she said. "*Apúrate.* Hurry up." She took the gun and reluctantly trained it on the other man. Every minute counted. She wasn't going to waste time arguing with a very determined and protective Beau.

The man with the helmet sat where Beau told him, on the opposite side of the patient from Sierra, not far from Beau. Beau took the pistol again and pressed it against the other man's side.

Sierra's memory was fuzzy about how to do a manual transfusion. She'd seen it done at her father's home when his men had needed emergency care but wanted to avoid a hospital and the questions their injuries might raise. But the man across from her whispered instructions and advice in his raspy, odd voice, guiding her through the steps. In just a few minutes the blood was flowing from him to their patient.

She sat back in relief. "Thank you—uh, maybe you could take off your helmet and introduce yourself?"

He remained silent.

"Answer the lady," Beau told him. "We'll find out anyway, once the police are here and you're taken into custody."

The helmet turned toward Beau. "And why would they do that?"

"Aiding and abetting fugitives. I recognize you. You helped the gunmen escape in the woods by my cabin earlier today. You're one of the drivers of the ATVs they used. And this guy is the one you punched."

Harsh laughter sounded from under the helmet. "I'm sure I don't know what you're talking about. You came up with that theory based on my clothing?"

"I've seen the faces of all these guys. They're the ones who attacked my house. I'm sure you know all about it since you knew about the kit in that SUV. You know the man lying here on the road, too, know his blood type. It's all connected."

"He's a friend. I've been in his SUV before."

"And you just happen to be in the woods while he and his other friends are shooting at us in my truck?"

"That's one way to look at it. The reality is far less damning. I was on my motorcycle while they followed me, heading to Mystic Lake for dinner at Stella's restaurant. I had to take a leak so I stopped and went into the woods. I have no idea why thcy decided to do what they did while I was in there." His hands fisted at his sides. "I really don't."

The genuine-sounding anger in his voice had Sierra wanting to believe his story. Except for one thing.

"Where's your motorcycle?" Beau asked the same question running through her mind.

"In the woods," he said. "And yes, I know that sounds suspicious. But I was worried there might be a bear in there and figured the sound of my motorcycle would clear out any critters so I could relieve myself without worrying about being attacked."

Beau shook his head, the skepticism heavy in his expression. "You have an answer for everything. But taken in totality, it sounds ridiculous. I don't believe any of it."

"Suit yourself. I'm only here because I'm hoping to save my friend."

Sierra pressed her fingers against the wounded man's neck again. Then she checked his pulse and respirations. "I think it's working. His pulse is stronger. He's breathing better. And unless I'm fooling myself, I think his color is improving."

Beau didn't look. He kept his attention, and his gun, focused on the man sitting beside him.

Helmet Guy pressed his palms against the road as if to steady himself. "I think you're right. He's not as pale as before." He suddenly weaved a little, tilting to the side.

Beau grabbed his arm, pushing him back to sitting. "Don't try to pull something. I'm not letting you get away."

Sierra noticed motorcycle guy's arms, which weren't covered by his shirt. "His color isn't right, Beau. I think we might have transfused too much." She reached for the tubing to clip it closed.

The man grabbed for her hand, but Beau knocked it away. "Don't touch her," he growled.

"Sorry, I just… I don't want her to stop. Give him a little more. I can handle it."

Sierra shook her head and clipped off the blood supply. "It's too dangerous for you. He's showing improvement. He has a much better chance than he did. We should go ahead and load him into our truck." She began removing the tubing and needles from both men. As soon as she finished wrapping a bandage around the motorcyclist's arm, Beau motioned for her to back up again.

"Sierra, grab the long gun and take it to the truck. I'll bring our patient in a minute."

"I should stay, keep an eye on him and—"

"He's holding his own right now." When she didn't move, he added, "Please."

She sighed heavily and picked up the incredibly heavy, odd-looking rifle that had done so much damage to the SUV. She hesitated, staring at the man in the helmet, wondering why he seemed so familiar.

"Sierra," Beau prodded.

"Okay, okay." She hurried to the truck and got inside.

"SHE'S GONE NOW," Beau said, as both of them stood. "You can stop with the fake raspy quality of your voice. Either take off the helmet or raise the visor so we can talk, man-to-man… *Esteban*."

Chapter Ten

A harsh laugh echoed from beneath the helmet. Turning his back to the truck, he lifted the visor. "How did you know? Even my own sister didn't recognize me." His voice was slightly accented now, similar to Sierra's accent, as he stopped trying to disguise it.

"That's because she's still grieving. She thinks you're dead and has no reason to suspect otherwise."

Esteban winced.

"Why aren't you?" Beau asked. "Dead? Or more to the point, why are you pretending to be dead, allowing her and the rest of your family to think that? And who's in the grave with your name on it?"

A loud, harsh sigh sounded through the opening in the helmet. "It's a long story. One neither of us has time for. You don't need to take Randy anywhere. I'll take care of him."

Not daring to turn his attention away from Sierra's brother, Beau watched Esteban as he listened to the wounded man's breathing. It seemed steady, unlabored, for now. But it wouldn't stay that way much longer, not without urgent medical care.

"I'm guessing you don't plan on transporting him on your motorcycle, if there even is a motorcycle."

"Oh, there is. I wasn't lying about that. I'll get some guys to take him soon."

"Soon? You have more thugs on their way here already?"

"I wouldn't call them *thugs*, exactly." He shrugged. "I called them as soon as you arrived."

"Called? Ah. You've been using a signal jammer. That's why we couldn't call for backup."

"I cover my bases." He motioned over his shoulder. "Sierra will be leaving with me. You might as well send her over here and get going. While you still can."

"Brave talk for a man with a gun pointed at his gut."

His mouth curved in a reluctant smile. "True enough. But my men would avenge me. Unless you want to be the cause of your own death, you won't pull the trigger. Time's running out, both for you and Randy. What's it going to be?"

"Why did you fake your death. Why did your men break into my cabin? And why did they try to kill me just now, even with Sierra here who also could have been killed?"

Esteban's smile faded. "There were going to be consequences for them putting her in danger. But your shootout solved that problem for me. They got jumpy while I was in the woods, started firing when they should have waited. Regardless, we didn't expect her to be with you. One of my men in town said he'd seen a cop take her into the jail. Another one saw the police chief's truck heading out of town. The plan was to surround you from both ends of this ridiculously long road. I wanted to take you hostage, to use you as a bargaining chip to get my sister out of jail." His hands fisted at his sides. "Like I said, things didn't turn out as expected. The group of guys I'm working with these days is unpredictable." He looked around. "What a mess. I don't know how I'm going to fix this. But first things first. I'm taking my sister with me."

Esteban suddenly ducked down and swept his leg out. But Beau anticipated his action. He dodged out of the way and slammed his fist into Esteban's jaw, spinning him around. Esteban managed to keep from falling, but he froze when Beau jammed the muzzle of his pistol against Esteban's forehead.

"One more move, one little twitch and it's lights-out, Covington."

Esteban stared at him, his dark eyes hot with rage. "You don't have a clue what you're getting into the middle of, here."

"Then, explain it to me. What's going on? Why did your father's men break into my cabin? Why are you in my town causing trouble?"

Esteban rolled his eyes, much like Sierra often did. "They're not my father's men. They're mine."

"Is there a difference?"

Esteban snorted. "You have no idea."

The distant sound of an engine had both of them tensing. Esteban's gaze darted toward the road behind Beau, confirming what that sound meant. His men were coming up the mountain from the direction of Chattanooga and would be here any minute. No doubt there were others coming in from the direction of Mystic Lake too. He and Sierra were surrounded. He had to get her out of here, fast. Dealing with her brother would have to wait for another time.

Beau backed up, still pointing his pistol at the other man. "Call your men. Tell them not to shoot at my truck. Call them, or die right here, right now. I'm out of patience."

"Damn it, lawman. I want my sister."

"Until I know why you're here and why you faked your death, I can't assume that you won't hurt her. She stays with me."

Esteban swore.

"Call them. Now."

"Okay, okay." He slowly pulled out his phone, eyeing Beau's pistol as he did. Then he punched in a number.

"Put it on Speaker mode. And speak in English," Beau warned.

Esteban ordered his men to stand down, to wait for him. Then he ended the call. "What now, cop?"

"Drop your phone. I don't want you calling them back and changing your orders the second I back away."

Esteban pitched it onto the road.

Beau brought his boot down hard on the screen, crushing it.

Esteban's jaw tightened. "You owe me a new phone."

"I'm sure you can afford to buy another one. Sierra and I are leaving. You and I will continue this conversation another day. In the meantime, if anyone harms one hair on her head, nothing will stop me from hunting you down. Understood?"

Esteban narrowed his eyes. "Why would you care what happens to her?"

"The same reason I care what happens to any innocent victim. I mean it. One hair."

"Same goes for me. You hurt her, copper, you die."

"I would expect nothing less from a *loving, caring* brother such as yourself who's led her to believe you're dead and whose men shot at her twice today." Sarcasm dripped from every word. An angry tic in the side of the man's jaw told Beau his barb had found its target.

"Lie down on the road with your hands behind your back," Beau ordered. "Don't get up until I'm gone."

The engine was louder now. The vehicle coming up from Chattanooga was dangerously close, probably around the next curve.

"Do it," Beau ordered, quickly backing toward his truck, his pistol trained on the other man.

Esteban flipped his visor down, then did as ordered, positioning himself with his head turned so he could watch Beau.

The muffled distant sound of a second engine whining up

the mountain from the direction of Mystic Lake had Beau swearing and racing the rest of the way to his truck. He hopped into the driver's seat, unsurprised to see that Sierra's brother had jumped up the moment his back was turned. He was running away from them, arms waving as yet another dark-colored SUV barreled around the curve toward them.

"*No dispares*," Esteban yelled. "Don't shoot."

Sierra stared at motorcycle guy, then shook her head as if trying to focus. "What happened between you two? What in the world is going on?" She clutched one of the other pistols that Beau had tossed in his backpack at his cabin and was aiming it through the hole where the windshield used to be, right at the SUV.

Hoping to avoid another barrage of gunfire, he grabbed the gun from her and set it in the console. "Get on the floor."

"What? No, I don't—"

"It's the safest place in the truck. The engine block should keep any bullets from hitting you if they fire at us."

She didn't move, clearly aggravated.

"Sierra—"

"Okay, okay. I know the routine," she snapped, turning around and sliding down into the footwell.

Beau sweated for a second, hoping the engine would still work after all the gunfire that had hit his truck. He blew out a breath in relief when it started right up.

He swung his truck around and floored the accelerator. It peeled out, the smell of burning rubber filling the cab as the truck shot down the road toward Mystic Lake.

Beau tossed the Kevlar vest on top of her.

She yelled in Spanish at him. Although he had no clue what she was saying, he was quite certain he didn't want to know. And dang if she wasn't adorable when she was ticked off. He had to bite his cheek to keep from smiling and risk whatever payback that might earn him.

As soon as they rounded the next curve, he braked, stopping the truck so quickly it rocked on its springs.

She grabbed the front of the passenger seat to keep from face-planting against it. "What's the problem now?"

"Phone." He had his in one hand and held his other hand out toward her. "Hurry."

"I don't understand. Why do you need—"

"Sierra, I'm trying to save your life. And mine. Please, give me your phone."

She reluctantly handed it to him.

He hurled both phones out the window toward the ravine on the far side of the road.

"Dang it, Beau. Was that really necessary?"

"No electronic trail, remember? Hang on."

She clutched the front of the passenger seat again as he slammed the gas pedal. He spun the wheel, sending the truck racing toward the other side of the road, the one where the forest marched up the mountain toward the sky.

"Hold on," he warned again. "Another sharp turn coming."

"Let me guess. You learned to drive watching those ridiculous *Fast and Furious* movies," she snapped.

He laughed and spun the wheel again, earning a few more swear words as the truck did a one-eighty and stopped on the shoulder of the road.

"Good grief," she muttered. "Tell me when I can open my eyes."

"Definitely not yet." He grinned and jammed the accelerator, skidding off the shoulder into a narrow rock-strewn area behind some boulders. If someone else drove down the road, it would be nearly impossible for them to realize there was a cut-through back there. Even though he'd known it was here, it had been hard for him to find it.

It was overgrown, by design. Little more than a path through the trees and barely wide enough for his truck to maneuver. Branches brushed the sides, making him wince at the sound of them scraping against metal, scratching the paint. Of course, that was nothing compared to the bullet holes and busted-out windshield. He was lucky the radiator hadn't been hit, or they'd have been stranded.

Once he couldn't see the road through the trees and bushes anymore, he pulled to a stop, and waited.

"Beau, what are we—"

"Sh," he whispered.

Her eyes flew open. Then she squeezed them shut again.

A full minute passed. Then the roar of a car rushing past them came from the road below. As soon as the sound of the engine began to fade in the distance, he sent his truck forward again, racing up the mountain. He rounded a switchback, then another, weaving back and forth heading higher and higher.

He risked a quick glance at Sierra to make sure she was okay. Her eyes were open wide now, and she was hanging onto both the front of the seat and the armrest on the door, her knuckles whitening because she was gripping so hard.

"What's going on?" Her voice was thick with a mixture of anger and fear. "What's happening? Why are all of those men after us? Did the injured man, Randy, did he die? Beau, please. Tell me something, anything."

Guilt rode him hard at the sound of the fear in her voice, the near desperation in her beautiful dark brown eyes. "I promise I'll explain soon. You can sit in the seat now. You're safe."

She struggled against the weight of the Kevlar vest to climb out of the footwell. He grabbed it and tossed it behind him. She crawled onto her seat and fastened her seat belt before lifting her head to look through the gaping hole where the windshield had once been. She gasped and pressed a hand to her throat.

"Safe? We're going straight up a mountain."

He chuckled. "It's not that bad. My truck couldn't make it up a grade that steep. That's why this road weaves back and forth, to give us a more gradual slope to climb."

"This isn't a road, it's a path for mountain goats." She let out a startled squeak as a small tree branch whipped through the hole, nearly hitting her.

"Good grief." She brushed leaves and twigs off her arms. "Assuming we don't end up falling off this mountain and we actually make it to wherever you're heading, where is that exactly? Where are we going?"

"Where I was hoping we wouldn't have to. Plan B."

Chapter Eleven

Sierra adjusted the straps of Beau's backpack she was wearing and glanced at him, standing a few yards away under a massive oak tree. She didn't know how he was managing their hike up the mountain with his large bag from the truck strapped across his back. It made her much smaller backpack seem paltry in comparison. And the man wasn't even breathing hard, dang it.

She leaned against an equally massive oak tree to the one where Beau stood, trying to catch her breath. It had probably been around since long before she was born. At any other time, she'd have treated it with reverence and awe, gaping up at the thick canopy overhead. But not today, or tonight really since the sunlight was rapidly fading. She clutched her aching side as she tried to recover enough to continue the grueling pace up the mountain that Beau had set.

"Plan B is going to kill me," she accused. "What's your goal? Hike the Appalachian Trail all the way to Maine?"

He grinned. "We haven't been hiking all that long in the grand scheme of things. We're almost there."

"Seriously? I feel like I've hiked a full marathon. Uphill. In heavy brush, with no real path to follow after you ditched your truck. And that amazing monster gun of yours. I still wish you'd held onto that."

"I didn't want to ditch the truck. Even with four-wheel drive there was no way it was getting through the thick forest up here. Next time, I'll take a Jeep or something similar. Or better yet, drive up the backside of the mountain. That's the easiest and best approach. But we didn't have a choice. As for that so-called monster gun, it's a SIG Sauer AR-15. And believe me, I hated to leave that behind too. But I ran out of ammunition for it. A heavy empty gun isn't worth toting, especially when I knew we had quite a hike to make. Hopefully I hid it well enough that I can come back and retrieve it later." He arched a brow. "You're still breathing hard. Are you okay?"

"What do you think? You've been driving me like the meanest of sheepherders. My legs are cramping. My side hurts. I'm thirsty and starting to get hangry."

"Starting?"

"Watch it or you'll find out just how mean I can be."

He lifted his hands in surrender. "Duly warned. It isn't much farther now. I'm hoping to get there before the sun sets. I don't want to have to use a flashlight since its light would be visible a long ways off."

His concerns had her stomach dropping with renewed worry as she glanced around. "Do you think they're actually in the mountains looking for us?"

"Count on it. But even if they eventually find my truck, they won't find our tracks or figure out that we used a tunnel under some boulders and popped up a hundred yards away. The tunnels in this area aren't on any official maps because they were never used for mining. They were created by moonshiners and smugglers decades ago, long before Mystic Lake was around."

Her breaths were coming easier now, her side barely hurting. She wiped the perspiration off her brow and straightened. "Then, how do *you* know about them?"

"The knowledge has been passed down through generations in my family. The land belongs to another family whose great-great-grandfather was best friends with my great-great-grandfather, on my mother's side." He glanced at the darkening sky. "You think you can hike a little bit farther now? There won't be much moonlight tonight to help us find our way once the sunlight's gone."

"How long? How much more torture do I have to endure?"

He shrugged. "Depends on how fast you can hike."

She frowned at him. "There had better be a soft bed, hot food and a solid roof over my head at the end of this ordeal."

"That might be expecting a bit too much, for today. I didn't realize I'd need this place anytime soon, so I didn't get to stock everything. But I promise there's a soft bed. And a solid roof."

"Food? Water? Come on, Beau. I haven't eaten since breakfast."

"I'll get supplies tomorrow. I can't feed you a hot meal. But I promise I won't let you go to sleep on an empty belly."

She grumbled beneath her breath.

"What was that?"

"Forget it. Lead the way. My blisters and I will trudge behind you at our own pace."

"Poor, Sierra. You'll be able to prop your feet up soon."

She shoved away from the tree. "Which way?"

He reached for her hand. "Want me to carry you?"

"Did you forget the hangry part?" She slapped his hand away. "I don't need anyone to carry me or coddle me. I can handle anything you can."

"I have no doubt. That way." He pointed.

"Up? Again?"

"Just over the next rise."

"Didn't you say that the last rise?"

"I really mean it this time."

She stalked past him, letting loose with a litany of insults in Spanish about his parentage, his upbringing and anything else she could think of to vent her frustration.

"Hey, now," he teased as he followed behind her. "I happen to know a few of those words. You're not being nice."

"And you're lucky you wouldn't let me take out one of those pistols you're hoarding in your backpack. Quit picking at me and acting like you're enjoying this miserable climb or so help me, I'll..." She continued her tirade in Spanish again, focusing on putting one foot in front of the other without tripping over a tree root or getting slapped in the face by yet another low-hanging branch.

The hardest part was trying to walk without limping. Her feet felt bruised and sore and burned when she walked, no doubt because of blisters. She hadn't exactly worn shoes for hiking. Not that she had *any* shoes appropriate for that kind of thing. She was just grateful that she'd changed into low-heeled leather shoes before they'd headed out rather than the spiked heels she'd had on when she'd first approached Beau at his home.

She lost track of time as she coaxed her aching muscles to keep climbing. But she was certain he was wrong about it not being much farther to finally reach their destination. Insects were buzzing or chirping or whatever it was called when the sun began to set at night. She wasn't exactly an outdoorsy type. And in spite of her exhaustion, she forced herself to speed up. She didn't want to be out here when it got completely dark any more than Beau did.

Maybe less than he did.

One of her many fears plaguing her today was that they might just be lost and Beau was pretending he knew where he was. Since her sense of direction was pretty much nonexistent, she didn't even want to contemplate being lost out here and having to rely on herself to find her way back to civilization.

"Sierra, you're limping. I really don't mind carrying you, at least for a little while, to give your feet a rest. I can shift my duffle bag to the side and you could climb on my back and—"

"No. I told you. I can handle anything you can."

He sighed and didn't ask again.

She steeled herself against the pain and tried harder to walk as normally as possible.

When they finally approached the crest of their most recent incline, she braced herself for disappointment. She fully expected that they'd head down the other side of this most recent mountain, or *hill* as Beau had teased so many times, and see that there was yet another rise to tackle before ending up wherever they were supposed to go. But when they reached the top, she froze. Not out of disappointment but out of astonishment.

Her eyes misted with unshed tears as she stared at the most beautiful sight she'd ever seen: a little log cabin with gleaming windows and what appeared to be a brand-new porch running across the front. The roof also looked brand-new and had rows of solar panels. A large propane tank off to one side along with those solar panels promised working electricity, which meant a hot shower. Or, if God was answering her prayers tonight, maybe even a long soak in a bubble bath.

When Beau stopped beside her, she looked up, searching his gaze. "Please. Please tell me we get to stop at this cute little cabin. I don't think I can make it any farther."

"This cute little cabin is our destination. Sierra Covington, welcome to Mystic Lake Police Department's first ever safe house. Welcome to plan B."

"I absolutely love plan B. As long as there's hot water—"

"There is. And all the windows have black-out blinds so we'll be able to use the lights without worrying that someone will see them. We'll have electricity, fresh hot coffee, bottled water and a few nonperishable snacks to tide us over."

"Snacks don't equal a meal, but everything else sounds far too good to worry about real food."

He squeezed her shoulder, smiling. "You're a trouper. Tomorrow, you'll have a real meal. Promise. Come on. Let's get you inside with those feet propped up."

She smiled in response, her mood lightening. Even the idea of the gunmen in the mountains looking for them didn't bother her. Not when she was about to get off her aching feet.

She started forward, then immediately fell to her knees, face heating with embarrassment. Her feet were so sore that stopping to stare at the house had been enough for them to give out on her when she'd tried to move again. She braced her hands on the ground to push herself to standing.

"*Pride goeth before the fall*," Beau said. "Isn't that the saying?"

She looked up at him. "What?"

"Never mind. Just don't hit me, okay?"

"Hit you? Why would I—oh!" He scooped her up and strode toward the cabin.

She automatically put her arms around his neck to hold on. Before she could decide whether to demand that he put her down or thank him for helping her, he was jogging up the stairs to the front porch.

"Mind keying in the code to the electronic lock for me?" He angled her near the keypad above the doorknob and told her the numbers to press.

The lock clicked. She turned the knob, and he pushed the door open with his boot, then headed inside, kicking it closed behind them. He didn't slow until he reached the surprisingly large sectional wedged into the small space, taking up almost all of two walls in the main room. Whoever had furnished the cabin hadn't been mindful of appropriately sized furniture.

As soon as he lowered her onto the couch, her criticisms for whoever had chosen it evaporated. That person was now her hero. The sectional was as soft as a cloud but with good support, pillowing her sore muscles and bruises as she settled back.

"Wow," she breathed. "This is the most comfortable couch ever."

"You're welcome."

"You selected it?"

"Yours truly. I figured if we ever actually needed a safe house it should be as comfortable as possible, a home away from home for someone in a stressful, tough situation. The bed is just as nice, with the right amount of firmness so you won't wake up with an aching back."

She'd just pushed her shoes off and was rubbing her aching feet when he said that. "Bed? Singular?"

"You don't want to share?"

She smiled her first real smile in hours. "I don't mind sharing a bed with a hot guy like you even a little bit. So if you're teasing, be careful. I'll call your bluff."

He chuckled. "Flattering, but not necessary. I can sleep on the sectional. As you've already found out, it's extremely comfortable. And long enough even for me. It pulls out to a bed as well, if I need it."

She sighed. "Your loss. If I wasn't so tired, I might try to change your mind. Honestly, I'm not even hungry anymore. I just want a bath and a bed at this point." She glanced toward the front door. "As long as you think it's safe?"

"Everything in this cabin was renovated with security in mind. The log walls will stop pretty much anything. The windows are bulletproof. The front and back doors are both solid steel. And I have a few tricks up my sleeve if we need to get out of here in a hurry."

"Sounds like you thought of everything, except for one very important thing." She straightened on the couch. "If you know about this place, then so do your officers. And the mayor, and city council I would expect. Maybe others, those who helped put that new porch and roof on. I'm not convinced this lovely cabin is actually a safe house, given all the people who know about it. Like you said, small town and all that. Everyone seems to know everything and everyone's business."

He sat down beside her. "Hopefully it will set you at ease to know that I considered those things when I first began searching for something we could use as a safe house. Without going into all of the details, I can assure you that I kept from creating a traceable electronic trail. The mayor and council aren't included among those who know the cabin's location. That was an agreement we made before I began hunting for property to purchase on behalf of the department. The only people who know about it are my officers and me. I trust them the way I'd trust my own family. Heck, more than my own family because they're law enforcement officers and know how important it is to keep this place a secret. None of them will tell anyone. Ever."

"What about the company that renovated it? And the company that delivered the furniture? Or the gas company that filled that tank outside?"

He cocked his head, studying her. "Have you always been this paranoid, or is it just because of what happened today?"

"Just because? Seriously? What happened today isn't enough to justify wanting to be absolutely certain that we're safe?"

"I was half teasing. Forget I said that. But, again, trust me that I thought through the potential of someone tracing the companies who furnished materials. It's because of that extra care that it took nine months to get all of the work done and the place furnished. No workers outside of me, my officers and one close friend have been here. The deliveries were made to another location and trekked in here by myself and the others I mentioned. My team and I put a lot of sweat equity into this place to do the improvements. That friend I mentioned is the one who supplied and filled the propane tank. He's someone I can count on to keep it filled without others knowing about it."

He motioned toward the front door. "As for physical security, that keypad controls steel bars that come in from the walls and floor to secure the door, which is in a steel frame connected to steel beams in the wall. Same goes for the back door. With enough force, someone on the outside could eventually break the windows. That's by design, in case there was ever a fire emergency. But they'd need heavy duty tools or something equivalent to do it. And we'd have enough warning to escape before they force their way in. Can I promise on my life that no one could ever figure out the location of this safe house and track us here? No. I can't. But it's unlikely. And you can consider me as your personal bodyguard. I'll do everything in my power to protect you."

She stared at him in wonder and shook her head. "I'm impressed. I really am. I don't know of any police department, or specifically police chief, who would have gone to all of that trouble and expense to keep some unknown future person safe. Your mayor is truly an idiot for letting you go."

He chuckled. "Thanks. As for the rest, I give a great deal of the credit to that friend I mentioned. He funded most of the cost out of his own pocket. If he hadn't, we still wouldn't have a safe house, not one I'd trust. Because, well, small town, small police budget."

"Who is this amazing friend? Does he have a name?"

"Actually, he's the same man who anonymously funded the town's medical chopper. But along with the rest of the secrecy about this place, his name will remain undisclosed."

"I guess that makes sense. You wouldn't want someone to trace his money to this place."

"Exactly. Now, if you're still interested in that hot bath, I'm happy to carry you to the bathroom. The house has a tankless water heater, so you'll have all the hot water you want."

In answer, she raised her arms.

He gently lifted her as before and carried her to the bathroom. When he carefully set her on her feet, he waited until she was steady before stepping back.

"Towels are in the linen closet. There are robes in there too. Toiletries, including toothbrushes and toothpaste, brushes, combs, things like that, are in that cabinet under the sink. And like any good safe house, the closet and chest of drawers in the connecting bedroom have new, unworn clothing in varying sizes. Mostly it's jeans, shorts and tops. And underwear is in the dresser—again brand-new, never worn. Hopefully you'll find what you need, at least for tonight. I can get one of my… one of the officers to bring you anything else you might need tomorrow. I'll actually update them tonight so they can get what you need ready for when they come up here, whichever officer ends up becoming our liaison. I'll leave that detail to Collier to decide."

"Sounds like you've thought of everything."

"If not, we'll rectify it later."

"What about you? I mean, clothes. Is there something here for you too?"

"The bag I hauled up here on my back from my truck doesn't just have extra weapons and ammo. It's my version of a go bag, with clothing and other items I might need for a few days. I'll shower once you're done. In the meantime, I'm going to walk the perimeter of the property, as a precaution. I'll check for signs of anyone sneaking around. But I don't expect there will be. This place is remote and a tough, long hike to get here, as you're aware. And about the only way to get through the rocks and boulders is that tunnel you and I used. Without the tunnel, someone coming up the mountain will eventually reach solid rock with no easy way around it. The hope is that they'll give up and turn around."

"Good to know."

He started to turn away but she stopped him with a hand on his arm.

He arched a brow in question.

She shook her head. "Hard to believe we only met this morning. In that time we've survived two shootouts. I survived a brief stint in jail. And somehow I survived running a marathon straight up a mountain," she continued.

"Exaggerate much?"

"Maybe a little. It's certainly no stretch to say that you've saved my life today. Although I honestly never expected someone would dare shoot at me, if they know about my father. Then again, I never expected Esteban to be murdered either."

He gently squeezed her hand as if to reassure her. "Shower, eat, rest. Tomorrow, we're going to dig into our investigation and figure out what's really going on."

After she closed the bathroom door, she reached into the pocket of her shorts and pulled out the item she'd pilfered from Beau's backpack when he'd been speaking to the motorcycle man.

A burner phone.

She slumped down to the floor and sat with her back against the wall, holding the phone and replaying everything in her mind that she'd seen. And heard. And felt. And she wondered…

When was Beau planning on telling her that her brother Esteban was alive?

Chapter Twelve

Beau set the last dish he'd dried in the cabinet, then raised the black-out blinds on the kitchen window over the sink, confirming what the time on his watch had indicated. The sun was coming up. Behind him, the sound of Sierra shifting in her chair at the table had him tossing the dishrag over the faucet and turning around.

"If you want more eggs, I can fire up the skillet again."

She shook her head. "I'm stuffed. That was the best egg-only breakfast I've ever had. Actually, it's the only egg-only breakfast I've ever had. But your expert seasoning made them delicious. I still can't believe you raided a neighbor's chicken coop to feed us. I'll bet that's the first law you've ever broken in your life."

"If we don't count the occasional speeding and foolish underage drinking in my misspent youth, you might be right. But I'll figure out a way to reimburse them later rather than leave money in the coop that would advertise that we're up here. Hopefully they'll figure a bear or something else in the woods scared their hens and that's why they don't have as many eggs to gather this morning." He motioned toward his laptop he'd set on the table earlier. "We don't have internet. But you can still document what you remember about the investigation you've done so far. And I've got a flash drive I loaded up in my office before we left yesterday. It lists all the drownings, boating accidents and people who've gone missing in the past few years. A hard copy of your brother's file is in my backpack too. We can compare notes and figure out our next steps in the investigation into his death."

"That would be hard to do since we both know he's not dead."

He stared at her in surprise. How long had she known? And why hadn't she said something earlier? Suspicions about her true intentions in involving him in all of this began to rear themselves again, suspicions he'd thought were already settled. Apparently not. "Your brother is alive?"

"Don't pretend you don't know. You recognized me from one of your law enforcement photographs after I told you my father's name. I'm sure you recognized Esteban too on the road. I saw him lift his shield up on the top of his helmet when he had his back to me and was facing you. You knew it was him. But you didn't tell me."

He shrugged, no longer bothering to deny it. "I never had a chance to tell you. We were on the run, then both of us crashed from near exhaustion after reaching the cabin. I was going to tell you today, rather than hit you with it last night. But I hadn't figured out how to tell you just yet. At this point, the real question is how long have you known? Hell, did you ever really think he was dead?"

"Seriously? I've been searching for his killer for months and you have the gall to ask me that?"

"Then, how did you know? You never saw his face on the road. He had his helmet on the whole time and his back turned to you when he lifted the face shield, as you said."

"I figured it out after we got here, at the safe house. I knew the guy with the motorcycle helmet seemed familiar, even thought of Esteban when I first saw him. But I discarded that idea as wishful thinking because I knew he was dead. But when I saw how he moved, how he ran, and heard him yelling at the men in that second SUV not to shoot, all the puzzle pieces started coming together in my mind. It wasn't until we got here and had a moment of peace to really think it through that I realized it had to be him, that the man in the motorcycle helmet is my brother. So I'll ask you again. What's the point of investigating anymore when we both know that he's alive? Why the pretense this morning?"

He blew out a long breath, then sat in the chair across from her. "Look, I'm sorry I didn't tell you earlier. I probably should have and—"

"Probably?"

"Definitely should have. I'm sorry."

She crossed her arms defiantly but seemed a little less aggravated at him.

"Can we chalk it up to it being a really, really bad day for both of us and move on?"

She rolled her eyes and uncrossed her arms. "Move on how? Where? I don't even see the point of an investigation now. I might as well find my brother and talk it out. That would be the quickest and easiest way to get the answers I want."

"And the most dangerous. Neither of us knows his involvement in the shootings yesterday. But he's definitely involved in some way, no question. He was one of the men picking up the gunmen from my cabin. And don't forget that he didn't exactly run out of the woods to call a halt to the shooting when his men in that SUV tried to kill us. The last guy, the one you transfused, was his friend. Randy. Remember? They were his friends, his men. Explain that."

She looked away. "I can't. But if I talk to Esteban—"

"And discover that Esteban is actually trying to kill you, you're dead."

Her eyes widened incredulously. "Why would you think he's trying to kill me?"

"I can't believe you even said that. He faked his death. You came here to look into it and suddenly people are shooting at you, the same people he knows well enough to transfuse in the middle of the road. Why would you think he *isn't* trying to kill you, or have you killed?"

"I don't have the facts to explain whatever is going on. But I know my brother. He's taken care of Rafael and me all our lives. He would never, ever hurt either one of us."

"And yet he always seems to be around when the bullets start flying."

Her eyes narrowed ominously. Before she could let loose with a tirade of words he probably wouldn't understand, he held up his hands. "Let's start over, all right? Obviously instead of investigating your brother's death, we now need to investigate why he faked it, who died in his place, and why someone's trying to kill us."

She crossed her arms again. "Fair enough. I guess."

"We need to compare notes. Decide our next steps. How long do you think it will take you to type up what you've investigated so far?"

"You're kidding, right? I've been here several months. There's no way I'll remember every place I've been, every person I've spoken to or eavesdropped on and what they said. It would be much easier, and faster, to sneak into my rental and download the files from my server. Or hook up to the internet somewhere to access my data in the cloud. It's a shame you don't have a satellite dish at the cabin or we could download my files right now."

"We can't risk leaving an electronic trail of any kind. No internet. Period. Someone could have already broken into your rental by now and is watching your cloud storage to trace any attempts at retrieval."

"It would take a computer genius to do that, don't you think?"

"I've done it before. Do you consider me to be a genius?"

The corner of her mouth lifted in a half smile.

"Don't answer that," he said. "I don't think my ego could handle whatever you're about to say. My point is that if I can do it, I imagine the men after us could as well. All it takes is a little digging on the internet to find out how. It's not that difficult."

"Then, it's going to be a long, tedious day of me having to rely solely on my memory to create a list of everything I've looked into."

"We've got the time. One of my former officers is going to bring us supplies today. They're coming up the mountain from the opposite direction that we did and will leave everything at a prearranged spot for me to retrieve later. Which reminds me, I need to tell them to include some soda for you. I didn't anticipate having a non-coffee-drinker in the safe house."

She scrunched up her nose. "Coffee is highly overrated. I don't understand the appeal."

He smiled and took a phone out of his jeans pocket.

She blinked. "I, uh, thought you threw your phone out when you tossed mine."

"I did. This is a cheap phone without a registered owner or contract, the type law enforcement calls a *burner phone*. I put some in my backpack at my old office yesterday. As long as we don't call someone whom the bad guys might try to trace back to us, it's safe to use."

He frowned at the screen. "That's odd. No cell service. I had service last night when I called Collier. I suppose a tower could be down. Then again, these phones are no frills, not always reliable. I'll try another one." He crossed to his backpack that he'd set on the table earlier and unzipped it.

"Ah, maybe *this* one will work," she said.

He looked up as she set one of the burner phones on the table. Her chin took on a defiant tilt. "Don't be mad. I was frustrated yesterday when you wouldn't share much information. I took it when you were standing on the road talking to… Esteban."

"When?" His voice was slightly hoarse as he tried to keep his anger from showing. He cleared his throat before continuing in a calmer tone. "When did you use it? Who did you call?" He took her phone and checked for cell service.

"Last night, right before bed after we snacked on peanut butter crackers."

He shook his head and checked the phone she'd given him. No bars on the screen. No service. He grabbed one more burner from the bag, the last of the three he had, and turned it on.

"Who did you call?" he repeated as the phone came to life. "Esteban?"

"Of course not. I don't know what phone number he's using after faking his death. I, uh…" She tapped her fingers on the tablc, broadcasting her nervousness. "I called Rafael, my other biological brother."

He jerked his head up, swearing.

"It was a quick call," she insisted. "I had to tell him not to worry if he heard anything on the grapevine about me. I didn't want him sending someone to look for me and getting in the middle of whatever is going on." Her chin raised again, her eyes flashing with resentment. "And I told him what you didn't tell me, that Esteban is alive."

Beau checked the screen, then tossed the phone into the bag

with the others. He strode to the front windows and flipped open the blinds.

Sierra hurried after him. "What's wrong?"

"What's wrong?" He didn't even spare her a glance as he studied the tree line fifty yards from the front of the cabin. "What's wrong is that by calling Rafael, you compromised our location. Which might not be a catastrophe except that I have no cell service this morning but had it last night. Sound familiar?"

Her eyes widened. She glanced past him outside. "You don't think—"

"Yesterday Esteban used a jamming device to block the cell service, preventing me from calling for backup. I'd bet every last penny I have that he's out there, right now, doing it again. He's here. His men are here."

Her eyes widened. "He jammed the service? He told you that?"

He gave her a curt nod. "Did you tell Rafael about the tunnel, the one we used to get to this cabin?"

"What? No, of course not." Her eyes flashed with anger. "Calling my brother may have been a mistake. But I didn't do anything to compromise our location. Not purposely or knowingly, anyway."

He didn't respond as he peered out the blinds again.

She looked back and forth. "I don't see anything. I don't see anyone."

"I don't either. I also don't hear anything. When I started cooking breakfast you mentioned the birds chirping, that they'd woken you up. Do you hear them now?"

Her hand shook as she pressed it to her chest. "No. Nothing. It's totally silent."

"Exactly. Something out there is scaring the birds. We're leaving." He strode to the table and grabbed the laptop. "Get one of the empty backpacks from the bedroom closet and stuff it with whatever clothing and toiletries you'll need if we have to camp out a few days. I'll give you two minutes."

"C-camp? Two minutes? Don't you think you're overreacting? There could be a bear out there scaring the birds. Or, or a—I don't know—some other animal that—"

Bam! Bam! Bam! Gunshots sounded from the woods, strafing against the windows.

She let out a startled gasp.

Beau yanked her behind the log wall.

"That glass might be called *bulletproof*," he said, "but it won't hold forever, especially if they use something more high-powered. Hurry. Get what you need."

She tore off through the cabin, almost colliding with the wall as she rounded the corner into the bedroom.

Beau flipped the front window blinds closed and then shut the ones over the kitchen sink. It was quiet again outside, no more shots. But that didn't mean the shooters were giving up. Whoever was outside the cabin meant business and was probably moving into position to flank them, surround them, if they hadn't already.

He grabbed his go bag from beside the couch and dropped it on the kitchen table beside his backpack. From the small pantry, he grabbed some of the energy bars and other snacks and shoved them into the pack. After tossing in some bottles of water, he zipped it closed.

Sierra ran into the kitchen area, her backpack strapped on.

A loud bang on the front windows had both of them turning around. It sounded as if someone was hitting the glass with their fist. A few seconds later, a muffled voice called out.

"Sierra, it's me. Esteban. Open the door. No one's going to hurt you."

She glanced up at Beau, her dark eyes full of indecision.

"No, Sierra," he warned. "Don't—"

She took off running.

He ran after her, backing up against the door to keep her from opening it. But she didn't head to the door. Instead, she flipped the blinds open on the window.

And stared into the eyes of her brother.

Esteban pressed the flat of his hand against the glass.

Sierra did the same from the other side with only the thickness of the windowpane separating them.

"I can explain everything," Esteban shouted to be heard through the window. "Open the door. We need to talk."

Beau grabbed her shoulders and turned her to look at him. "We can't trust him, Sierra. God knows I'd love to prove that your brother doesn't want to hurt you. But every time the bullets start flying, who shows up? Esteban. The one who let you think he was dead. And now that you know otherwise, he's again with men who are shooting at us. Think. Use that beautiful brain of yours. Are you willing to bet your life that you can trust him?"

She looked back at the window. Her brother still stood there, peering through the blinds, an imploring look on his face.

"I'm not asking you to condemn him or even hate him," Beau continued, "or turn your back on him forever. I'm asking you to be careful, to not risk your life again by hoping he can control the men he hasn't managed to control before. There are two possibilities here. Either he wants you dead—" he held up a hand to stop her when she began to argue "—or he wants to protect you against whatever's going on. Either way, he's already proven, over and over, that he can't keep you safe. I've proven the opposite. I can, and will, protect you. No matter what. But you have to trust me."

The window thumped repeatedly as her brother slammed

his fist against it, his face scrunched up in anger. He abruptly stopped and yelled, “Sierra, don’t trust the cop.”

Beau wanted to throw open the door and slam his fist against the man’s jaw. Instead, he forced a calmness he was far from feeling into his voice and focused on the woman whose life he knew, without a doubt, was in imminent danger. He just didn’t know why.

“I can get us out of here. Come with me, Sierra. Let’s find the truth together.”

She squeezed her eyes shut, her body trembling as she hesitated. The pounding and shouting started again, startling her. She turned away from the window, away from her brother, and faced Beau again.

“Sierra,” Esteban yelled, his voice muffled through the thick glass. “Sierra, come with me. I’ll protect you, explain everything.”

Beau flipped the blinds closed, his large warm hand gently grasping hers.

She flinched with each pound of her brother’s fists. “Okay. Okay. I’ll go with you, but only so I can prove you wrong about my brother. Hopefully Esteban will forgive me one day for literally turning my back on him.” Her voice choked on the last word.

Unable to resist the urge to offer comfort, he pulled her into his arms, not even sure she’d let him. But she did. More than that, she melted against him, a sob escaping her as she turned her face against his chest.

Beau whispered in broken Spanish against the top of her head as he tried to soothe her. It was as if the world outside, the danger on their doorstep, faded away as he held her. All he wanted to do was take away the grief and fear he’d seen in her eyes, take away the hurt she felt over her brother’s betrayal. And over Beau's betrayal in not telling her earlier what he'd found out, that her brother was alive.

Knowing he shouldn't, but helpless not to, he pressed a whisper-soft kiss against her dark silky hair. When she only held him tighter, he realized they both were in trouble. The danger, the trauma, everything that had happened since they'd met had woven a tenuous bond between them. And now he was doing what he'd told her not to do: feeling, letting his emotions guide his actions instead of his head.

He forced himself to gently push her back. Guilt rode him hard as the sound of Esteban's fists against the window finally caught his attention again. They'd spent precious seconds standing there, comforting each other. Time that could mean the difference between life and death.

"We're wasting time. We have to go." His voice came out harder than he'd intended, and the words were all wrong.

She jerked back, turning away, but not before he saw the hurt in her eyes.

He shook his head. Nothing was going as planned. He wanted to protect this woman. Instead, he'd hurt her. And he was making poor decisions. He'd have to be far more careful to guard himself against the attraction he'd tried to deny until now. If he didn't, he'd continue to make foolish decisions.

Like standing here even one more second when she was in danger.

He shrugged his backpack on, then leaned past her and grabbed his go bag, slinging the strap crosswise over his chest.

Pounding sounded on the front door now instead of the window, along with more muffled shouts from her brother.

A single tear coursed down her cheek. "Maybe I should—"

Bam! Bam!

Bullets pinged off the log walls of the cabin.

Her brother's bellow of rage sounded from outside. The shooting immediately stopped.

Sierra's face turned so pale it was as if her beautiful dark Spanish skin—no, Cuban skin—had turned white. "He stopped them," she whispered, defending her brother. "He stopped them from shooting again."

Beau sighed heavily. "He stopped them, yes, but only after they shot at us. Like before. Until he can consistently control them, we still need to go."

"Right. Yes. But, where, how—"

"Remember I told you I had a few tricks up my sleeve if we needed to leave in a hurry?"

"I remember."

He took her hand in his and led her into the small pantry that was barely a walk-in. He pulled a fake shelf support down and to the side. A loud click sounded, and the back wall pulled toward them, leaving a narrow opening.

"What is it?" she said. "One of those safe rooms where people hide from burglars?"

"Even better. It's essentially a bolt-hole, like they had centuries ago so people could escape unseen when a castle was besieged."

"Oh, we have something like that at my father's mansion. It goes out into the woods behind the house. But Daddy said it's in case there's a fire."

Beau chuckled. "I'll bet that's what it's for. Not so he can get away if law enforcement ever manages to close in on him."

"Be nice."

He sighed. "Anyway, like I was saying. A ladder is attached at the edge of the tunnel opening. Solar-powered lights will come on as soon as we reach the bottom."

"No flashlight this time? Like the one from your backpack in the earlier tunnel?"

He smiled at the memory of her swearing at the low light from the flashlight he'd used before. "This little cabin has all the modern upgrades."

"Except internet."

He laughed, amazed he could do so in spite of what was going on.

A much louder thumping sounded behind them, repeating over and over. The floor shook, ever so slightly, but enough to dislodge a box of cereal from one of the shelves. Beau managed to catch it before it could fall on Sierra's head.

Her eyes widened. "What are they doing now?"

"Sounds like they're trying to break down the door." He tossed the box on one of the lower shelves. "I wouldn't think it's possible without heavy equipment. But it sounds like they're using a log or something really heavy. We have to go. Now. Hurry, Sierra."

As soon as she safely reached the bottom of the ladder and the tunnel's lights came on, Beau closed the outer pantry door. Then he stood on the ladder and closed the second door, the one that led down into the tunnel. He secured three iron bars across the door, resting the ends in thick hooks bolted into the framing on the wall. Then he jumped down the last few steps, grabbed Sierra's hand and started running.

Chapter Thirteen

A patch of light up ahead had Sierra wondering if they were literally, finally, reaching the light at the end of the tunnel or whether it was yet another cruel trick of her mind. Since they'd entered the tunnel beneath the cabin, she'd thought they were nearing an exit many times only to discover it was yet another ventilation shaft. The small square of sunlight had fooled her so many times that she couldn't even get excited about this next one up ahead, even though it seemed much larger.

"Almost there," Beau told her as he kept his strides shorter for her benefit, sticking to her side like glue.

He'd encouraged her every time she'd faltered. Kept encouraging her to drink to stay hydrated, even in the coolness of the mine shaft. He'd warned her that the mind can play tricks down here, like making her think she wasn't thirsty because of the temperature. But not staying hydrated with all the walking and jogging they were doing could make her muscles cramp up. Of course, pushing her to drink had its drawbacks too. She'd had to stop earlier around a corner to relieve her bladder. It grossed her out not having bathroom tissue and having to pee on the dirt. She felt dirty and disgusting while Beau never seemed to break a sweat or get tired.

She kind of hated him for that.

Her silence must have made him worry because he gently

pulled her to a stop. "What's wrong? Another leg cramp? I can massage—"

"No way." She jerked back, not wanting him to touch her. She was so dirty and sweaty her face flushed with embarrassment at the thought of him even being close to her.

At his questioning look, she sighed. "Nothing's wrong, other than I desperately need a shower and a fresh change of clothes. Oh, and the fact that gunmen may or may not be following us. And that my own brother may or may not want me dead for reasons unknown."

He looked so handsome and unaffected by everything happening that she wanted to punch him. Or kiss him. No, not kiss him. Not in her current state. She switched back to resentment and wanting to punch him.

"Remember those yummy fresh eggs we had for breakfast?" he asked.

She drew several deep breaths, trying to slow her racing heart. She'd always considered herself fit. Apparently, she wasn't. There were visions of Pilates and yoga in her future, if she survived long enough to leave Mystic Lake.

"Yes, of course I remember the eggs. Why?"

"Because that fine family's little farm where I pilfered those eggs isn't far from the tunnel exit up ahead. If you can hold on just a little longer we'll soon be at their place. I distinctly remember several cars near their farmhouse. I'm certain that once I offer amends for the eggs and explain that we need assistance, they'll be happy to drive us off this mountain."

She glanced down the tunnel. "When you say something isn't far, that's my warning that I'm in for another long hike. Apparently you have no concept of actual distances. But what did you mean about the exit up ahead? That next patch of light isn't a ventilation shaft?"

"Not this time. It's the real deal. The end of our journey. Well, except for a short hike to the farm of course."

She groaned. "Your short hikes are half-marathons."

"It really isn't that much farther. Promise." He glanced behind her down the long, dimly lit tunnel that led back to the cabin. "I haven't heard anyone behind us this entire time. But I can't imagine they'd give up until they figure out where we went. We need to get going. I can carry you on my back if you want and—"

"No, no way. I'm filthy."

"You're beautiful even with a little tunnel dirt. I don't mind carrying you."

She ignored the ridiculous burst of pleasure inside her at his compliment. He didn't mean it. He couldn't, not in her current level of disgusting.

She held out her hands to stop him when he took a step toward her. "I'm fine. Really. You let me rest long enough this time so that I'm not miserable. And your carrot of catching a ride down the mountain along with the stick of the gunmen still looking for us is enough to get me going again. Lead the way."

In spite of her words, he did as he always did. Instead of leading he walked beside her, constantly on alert for dangers both in front of and behind them. If the man hadn't been a cop, she'd swear he was perfect. But unfortunately, that didn't make him perfect for her. There could never be anything permanent and lasting between her and a man like him. They were from two completely different worlds.

Even though she'd strived her entire life to stay away from any of the questionable things her father and his sons did—admittedly including her two biological brothers to a lesser degree—it was impossible to steer clear of their bad reputations. They tainted her own reputation, making people assume the worst no matter how hard she tried to prove she wasn't like the others.

Of course, she really only had herself to blame. She'd made her own choices in life. If she'd left her family as soon as she'd gotten old enough to realize there were shady things going on, she could have lived a life on her own that wasn't overshadowed by theirs. But leaving wasn't something she'd been willing to do. She loved them, in spite of everything. And she refused to give them up regardless of the consequences to herself.

Well, unless one of them actually was trying to kill her.

Her shoulders slumped as the questions about Esteban swirled around in her mind. But there were no answers. Not yet. And until she got those answers, she'd be torn about what to do about him.

"Stop right there," Beau whispered when they reached the tunnel exit, obscured by stones and a boulder just like the other tunnel they'd used on their way to the cabin. "Let me scout it out first. I don't expect your brother and his men would have figured out about this tunnel yet or made their way through the forest this far searching for us. But I never expected them to find the cabin in the first place. It's best to be extra cautious."

He took off his go bag, then his backpack and set them on the ground beside her. Crouching down, he unzipped the backpack and rummaged inside, grabbing an extra magazine of ammunition for his pistol. Then he jerked his head up, frowning at her.

"Really, Sierra? You took one of my guns?"

"You have two more in there. Plus the one you always have holstered at your hip. I didn't see why you couldn't share." She pulled the right leg of her jeans up revealing the pistol in the ankle holster.

He shook his head and stood, pocketing the extra magazine. "You do realize it's loaded, right?"

"*Pfft.* Of course. I wouldn't have taken it, otherwise."

"What's rule number one?"

"What are we, fifteen? Prepping for the SATs?"

"If you prepped for your college entrance exams at fifteen, you're the true genius here. Rule number one?"

She rolled her eyes. "Never point a gun at someone in law enforcement."

"And rule number two?"

"Don't point a gun unless I'm prepared to shoot whoever's on the other end. No bluffing. Do I get a lollipop now for passing my test?"

"You don't need a pistol, Sierra. You're already a pistol. You know that?"

She batted her eyelashes. "You say the sweetest things."

He laughed. "You really are something."

"So I've heard."

He took his pistol out of the holster on his belt, holding it down by his side. Seeing it in his hand, knowing why he had it out, sobered her and tamped down her urge to tease him again. Having people wanting them dead was a definite mood killer.

"Stay here, Sierra. Keep that gun handy and don't hesitate to use it if those men discover the tunnel entrance, or if you hear anyone behind you in the tunnel. I won't be gone long. Before I come back inside, I'll call out and let you know it's me."

With that, he disappeared around a curve in the rock wall.

Sierra took the gun from her ankle holster and held it down by her side the way she'd seen Beau do so many times. She sure didn't want it to be holstered if she suddenly needed it. But she'd keep his rules in mind and be careful about pointing it unless she was positive that she needed to.

She leaned back against the rock wall and settled in for a

long wait. After all, Beau had proven his estimates of times and distances were always way off. If he was back within an hour, she'd be surprised.

"I'm back, Sierra," a familiar deep voice called from outside the entrance.

She blinked and stared at the patch of sunlight and the rocks behind it. "Beau? You've only been gone a few minutes."

"Circumstances changed. Before I come in, remember rule number one?"

"We already had this conversation earlier."

"And I know darn well your first instinct when it comes to guns. Lower your gun, Sierra, before I come inside."

She frowned and looked down. Sure enough, she'd instinctively aimed the gun at the tunnel entrance as soon as she'd heard his voice, a split second before she'd realized it was him. She quickly shoved it into the waistband of her jeans to keep it close, just as Beau rounded the corner.

He shook his head when he saw the gun sticking out.

She was about to make a sarcastic comment but stopped when she saw that he wasn't alone. She reached for her gun again.

Beau grabbed it before she could aim it. "Good grief, Sierra. I warned you that I was coming inside. And to remember rule number one."

"I wasn't going to aim it at *you*."

"What about my officer? You didn't notice her uniform?"

"I'm noticing it now."

The attractive woman beside him with skin and hair that was darker than Sierra's glanced back and forth. "Uh, is there something going on here that I should be aware of? An inside joke, or what?"

"Who are you?" Sierra asked, not in the mood for unnecessary conversation.

Beau motioned toward the other woman. "This is officer Liza Fletcher. She used to work for me—"

"Still do, as far as I'm concerned," Fletcher said. "If the mayor thinks I'm going to call anyone else *Chief*, especially that idiot Kevin Sumner that he wants to hire, he's in for a huge disappointment." She stepped forward and held out her hand. "You must be Sierra Covington. Pleased to meet you."

Sierra stared in surprise at the officer's hand before shaking it. "Um, nice to meet you too. What's going on, exactly? I thought Beau was paying for the eggs and bumming a ride off the mountain."

Fletcher's friendly brown eyes widened as she glanced at Beau. "Paying for eggs? Bumming a ride?"

He gave her a pained look. "I'll explain later. Sierra, Fletcher came here to bring us supplies. But since our circumstances have changed, we're hitching a ride with her. We should—"

Sierra grabbed his hand and tugged him toward the end of the tunnel. "Which way to the car?"

Chapter Fourteen

Beau set his laptop on the coffee table in front of one of two couches forming an *L* in the living area of the new cabin where he and Sierra were staying now. On the far wall was a big-screen TV, framed by two large windows with the morning sun peeking through slits in the blinds. He clicked the remote, turning it on. The meeting was planned to start soon so he brought up the meeting software and began the log-in process. When he heard footsteps, he glanced toward the opening to the hallway.

Sierra rounded the corner, padding across the hardwood floor in pink ankle socks. But it wasn't the socks that had his breath hitching in his throat, it was those long slim legs encased in tight blue denim that made his body harden uncomfortably. And her curves revealed by the low cut white blouse that highlighted the gorgeous color of her skin. He was going to have to tell Fletcher to order Sierra more clothes that didn't reveal so much or flatter her curves so well. Heck, who was he kidding? She could be wearing a sack from neck to ankles and she'd still be gorgeous.

She stopped a few feet away. Then her lips curved in a sexy smile. "You like?" She winked.

He cleared his throat and tore his gaze away from her, focusing instead on the laptop. "Did Fletcher manage to get everything you needed?"

She huffed as if in disappointment and plopped down on the couch beside him. "She did an amazing job. Even the leather loafers fit perfectly. I still can't believe she managed to order all of those clothes the night we reached the safe house, overnighted them to her home, then already dropped them off here at the cabin this morning. That was so sweet of her."

"It's her job. You're a protected witness while our investigation is in progress. She'll be reimbursed by the department."

"Well, still. It was nice of her to go to all that trouble. And how she guessed my sizes so well is beyond me. Maybe she went online and looked at pictures of me with my family or something."

He cleared his throat. "Or, after you went to bed last night, I checked your sizes in the laundry basket and passed that information to her. I wouldn't have done it, but she pushed me, saying she needed the exact sizes or I'd have to wake you. I almost did wake you, but you'd conked right out and seemed exhausted. I apologize for the invasion of privacy of looking through your clothes. It seemed like the best decision at the time. But you may feel otherwise."

She bumped him with her elbow. "You're sweet to worry. But I don't mind at all. Having showered, slept and now wearing clean clothes makes up for everything. I don't think I'll be cranky at all today."

He started to teasingly disagree, but her warning look had him keeping his mouth firmly shut.

"You know," she continued, "I'd have been fine with us sharing the bed last night if you'd wanted to instead of you sleeping on the couch. I'm fine sharing it tonight if you want." She gave him a suggestive look.

He couldn't help but laugh. "Careful, Sierra. I might take you seriously sometime and call your bluff."

"Oh, honey. It's not a bluff. Call it. I dare you."

The sound of laughter had both of them looking up at the TV screen. Beau groaned when he saw that his team had joined the online meeting already.

Fletcher grinned and leaned close to the camera. "I'd say get a room, you two, but you already have that cabin all to yourselves." She giggled, and Collier grinned right along with her. Officer O'Brien, his other female officer, rolled her eyes at her fellow officers as if they were misbehaving children. Beau wished he was still the chief right this minute. He'd have given her a big fat bonus for being the only mature one in the room.

Sierra crossed her legs on the couch cushion and settled back as if their teasing didn't bother her in the slightest.

It probably didn't.

"Officer Fletcher," she said, "thanks again for the clothes. It makes being cooped up in a rental cabin with Beau that much more bearable. And thanks, sincerely, for getting us such a nice place to stay. I didn't even know they had cabins this large and fancy right on Mystic Lake or I'd have rented one myself."

Fletcher grinned. "Yeah, I see you're really suffering there. You're extremely welcome for the clothes. As to the cabin, the chief, as in Chief Dawson, is the one who arranged the rental, including the boat at the dock out front. One of his friends out of town rented it on his behalf so there wasn't a way to trace it electronically back to the police, or you specifically."

Beau tapped his hand on the coffee table. "If you two are finished becoming fast friends, I'd like to get this meeting started."

"Don't be so grumpy, Beau." Sierra patted his thigh.

He winced even before he saw the shocked looks on his former officers' faces. He'd never tolerated such teasing or familiarity from anyone else. But he'd failed miserably in making Sierra respect him and treat him the way he was used to as an officer of the law. Or at least treat him seriously instead of so cavalierly.

He cleared his throat again. “Sierra Covington, you’ve met Officer Fletcher of course, and Officer Collier beside her. The third officer is O’Brien. They’re in a room at Stella’s B and B so there wasn’t any worry about it potentially being bugged or any hidden cameras. The last officer who used to work under me is Ortiz. He’s manning the police station right now and couldn’t be on the call.”

“Let’s see,” Sierra said. “So it’s Liza, Chris and—I’m sorry, what should I call you, Officer O’Brien?”

“You’ll call them Officers Fletcher, Collier and O’Brien,” Beau instructed. “And if you ever speak to my fourth officer, it’s Officer Ortiz.”

Sierra frowned at him. “Fine. I can do that. But how long have you known them that you still use their last names?”

Collier’s eyes widened.

Fletcher laughed.

O’Brien smiled, barely.

“It’s called *respect*,” Beau said. He waved his hand in the air. “Enough of this nonsense. Let’s address the issues at hand, specifically the shooting at my home and the subsequent shootings on the main exit road and at the safe house. But before that, I know Collier was acting chief initially. But has the mayor appointed you officially as acting chief or are you all sharing those duties going forward? At least until Sumner comes on board.”

Collier grimaced. “I hope that never happens. As for officially in charge, that would be me. No one else wanted the job.”

Fletcher rolled her eyes. “He’s being modest. I hate to even say this out loud around him, but we all know he’s our best option right now.”

Collier blinked. “A compliment? From you?”

"Don't get used to it."

Collier grinned.

"Congratulations," Beau said. "I'm sure you'll do a fine job. I assume you updated the mayor about the recent events. What did he have to say about it?"

Collier's neck flushed a dull red. "Um, not much. He said to keep him informed if I needed anything."

Beau stared at his former officers, noting that all of them seemed uncomfortable. His stomach sank. "Please tell me I'm wrong in thinking that none of you reported the shootings to your *boss*, the mayor?"

Collier straightened. "As acting chief, it was my opinion that keeping this as quiet as possible until we knew the mayor's role in it was the best course of action."

"Until you knew the mayor's role? What the heck, Collier? What are you basing that suspicion on?"

He motioned to the others. "We discussed the secret meeting he arranged at the station, the one where he tried to fire you. And everything else going on. We're all in agreement, including Danny—Officer Ortiz. Something doesn't smell right. We've added the mayor to our list of people who need to be investigated to see if he's received some kind of outside pressure to railroad you out of a job."

"Well, of course he has. It's called an *expensive lawsuit*, and *being fiscally responsible.* Tanya Jericho's parents have launched a multimillion dollar lawsuit against our town. If you were the mayor and you discovered you could get the lawsuit settled for a fraction of that amount if you got rid of the police chief, what would you do?"

Collier's jaw set. "Not what you think I'd do, apparently. I wouldn't throw an innocent man to the wolves, let alone one who has done so much for our community, just to avoid going to court over a frivolous lawsuit that should have been dismissed the moment it was filed. Whether you agree with me or not, *Chief*—and I mean that, you're still the chief in my eyes—that's our decision. All four of us. We're going to get justice for you, Ms. Covington and our town. And it won't be at the expense of people who've done absolutely nothing wrong."

"Way to go, Chris." Sierra did a fist pump.

Beau slowly turned his head to look at her. "Just when did you get a personality transplant and start being so warm and cozy with *cops*?"

She rolled her eyes. "I guess since one of them got me nice clean clothes, a soft bed and a warm shower. Being with you is teaching me that not all cops are bad. But, hey, if it really bothers you, I'll be more formal. Way to go *Officer Collier*." She winked.

"*Ms. Covington*, maybe you should retire to your room for the duration of this meeting."

She crossed her arms, all signs of amusement gone. "Not a chance in hell, *Chief Dawson*. And don't talk down to me like I'm a child or one of your officers. This is my future we're going to discuss, my safety. And yours. I'm not going anywhere."

The suddenly tension-filled silence was interrupted by Collier. "I'll go ahead and provide an update on the progress of our investigations since the first shooting that occurred. Is that okay with you, Chief?"

Beau didn't even bother to correct Collier for calling him *Chief* again. Instead, he sat back and crossed his arms. "By all means. Go right ahead, Chief Collier."

Collier's brows rose, but he picked up a printed report and began reading it, explaining what each of them had been doing and what leads had been followed. In short, although they'd collected a lot of evidence at the first two sites, they hadn't caught any of the men after them and had no real leads as to their identities, other than that the leader appeared to be the brother who Sierra had believed to have been killed a year ago. They also, so far, hadn't been able to identify any of the dead men from the roadway shootout.

"I'm prepared to call Sheriff Galloway in Chattanooga and ask him to send deputies tomorrow morning to assist with a search of the safe house area," Collier said. "But doing so would require that I notify the mayor first. I can handle that, no problem. But being upfront about this situation means also revealing that the Covington family, at the very least Sierra and Esteban, are involved. If that news gets out, I predict that Mystic Lake will be overrun with Feds from every agency you can imagine in a matter of hours. I don't have to tell you what that would do to our own investigations."

Beau tightened his fists. "It would shut them down, cold. The Feds would turn this into an all-out effort to catch Michael Covington and put him out of business rather than focusing on Esteban's role and why he's here in Mystic Lake." He eyed Fletcher, O'Brien and Collier. "You three have already made up your mind, haven't you? You're not calling the sheriff. And you're not telling the mayor."

This time it was O'Brien who spoke up. "As a former FBI agent myself, I can verify that what Chris just said is the absolute truth. Bring in anyone from the outside at this point and you'll never find the truth behind what's going on in Mystic Lake. Why? Because no one outside of our town cares. They're all about bringing down organized crime. I get that. It's a noble goal. But they've been after Mr. Covington for decades. I haven't seen anything recently that makes me think they'd have any better chance at bringing him down now, if they come here investigating, than they've done in the past. It's my opinion that we'd come out of this with absolutely no useful answers, no arrests, nothing. And both you and Ms. Covington would be in as much danger, limbo really, not knowing who to trust, as you are right now."

Beau blinked in surprise at the feel of Sierra's hand closing around his. He looked at her, fully planning on pulling his hand away and telling her to focus on the meeting and stop playing around. But when he saw the fear in her eyes and that she was staring at the TV screen, he realized she wasn't playing.

She was terrified.

While he didn't return the gesture by squeezing her hand, especially with his team watching, he didn't pull away either. He looked back at the TV and pretended he didn't want to pull Sierra into his arms and try his best to chase her fears away.

"Collier, what's your plan?" he asked.

The three of them looked at each other before he answered. "We know we can't keep this a secret for long, a few days at most. There are already mumblings in town about people hearing gunshots. Fletcher put out a cover story about poachers and an accident on the main road to explain the debris after we quietly hauled away that SUV and did our best to get the area rinsed down. But people will talk. The truth will come out. We need to do everything we can in the next forty-eight hours to delay that. But more importantly, we need that time to dig in and get as much information as we can before all hell breaks loose."

"That's as apt a description as I've heard so far. All right. If you're looking for my blessing, I'm afraid I can't give it. Not telling the truth, hiding any of this, puts all of your careers in jeopardy. So the decision is entirely yours, as a team, including Ortiz."

"We're all in agreement," Collier said. "We already voted on it earlier. The result was unanimous. We want all five of us, including you, Chief Dawson, to resolve this together or go down together. Fighting. And even though I'm acting chief, that's just for show, for the mayor and the city council. We're looking to you for direction. Give us our marching orders, Chief."

Beau shook his head. "I never realized you were this stubborn, Collier. All right, then. We do this together. As a team. Buckle up. It's going to be a fast, bumpy ride. I'm tired of running."

"So am I," Sierra said, still clinging to his hand.

He gave in to the impulse and lightly squeezed her hand in response and gave her an encouraging smile, in spite of the officers watching. "No more running. No more hiding. It's time to go on the offensive."

Nearly an hour later, Beau ended the call and turned off the TV.

"We need to talk." Sierra crossed her arms.

He drew up one knee to face her as he rested an arm across the back of the couch. "You don't agree with everyone's assignments? I could see you weren't exactly thrilled when we discussed our plans for today."

"Honestly, I'm not thrilled about any of this. In spite of my earlier teasing, associating so closely with police and trusting them to actually help me doesn't come easily. Not that I have anything against law enforcement in general. It's just that they've always been so aggressive in their pursuit of my family that I don't exactly trust them to have my best interests at heart."

He considered that. "I understand your concern."

"No. I don't think you do."

"Then enlighten me."

She let out an impatient breath. "I appreciate what your people are doing, in theory, if they really do dig for information and pound the pavement or whatever they called it, trying to get a lead on any nonlocals hanging around the area. And them looking for clues up at the safe house to try to pick up the trail. Researching the SUV to see if they can figure out where it came from, who owns it, all of that. And checking the vacation cabins in the mountains to see which ones show signs of four-wheelers being in the area and—"

He laughed and held up his hands. "If you're trying to prove that you paid attention, I believe you. You listened to the discussion and understand what each person is going to do today. Trust issues aside, what's bothering you?"

"You."

His smile faded. "Me? You don't trust me?"

Her eyes widened. "No, no. I mean, yes. I do. Well, as much as I can trust any cop. I was getting nowhere on my own and was desperate for help. I slogged through the internet for weeks for background information on you before I decided to risk approaching you."

"Basically you don't trust me because I'm a police officer, or was one, and—"

"Once a cop, always a cop. Kind of like the Marines."

"Maybe you're right about that. Regardless, what you're telling me is I'm the lesser of evils and you wouldn't have come to me if you believed you had any other option. Is that accurate?"

She rolled her eyes. "Don't get all defensive. You know my situation, my background. It was beyond difficult going to you. But I did. And I don't regret it. You've saved my life over and over and risked your own each time, for no reason other than you're one of those really good people that is so rare these days."

"You make me sound like a dang Boy Scout."

"Were you? A Boy Scout?"

"That's not the point. What's the problem, Sierra? What do

you want me to do to make you feel more comfortable with how we're approaching the investigation?"

"Take me with you."

He stared at her, then shook his head. "No. We agreed you would stay here when I go out."

"No, you and your team agreed. I wasn't consulted about being told to stay put. I want to be an active participant in the search for the truth."

"You've been investigating for months with no progress. It's my turn to give it a try, which would be much easier without me worrying about your safety. I need you here, in the cabin, with a locked door, a gun—although the thought of that actually scares me—and an emergency phone. Keeping you out of sight is the best way to ensure your safety."

"Let's go back to your comment that I've been investigating for months and now it's your turn." She tilted her head in that defiant angle that was becoming all too familiar. "You investigated the alleged drowning of Jake Randolph, aka my brother, for months. And you came up with nothing."

"Ouch."

She took his hand in hers again, her soft skin doing alarming things to his pulse.

"Beau, in case you haven't noticed, I'm not good at subtlety or sugarcoating things. I tell it like it is. But I'm not trying to criticize you. I'm really not. I'm trying to say that, separately, neither of us were successful in figuring out what my brother was up to. It only makes sense that to view things in a new light, to make real headway, we need to work together. Be the yin for each other's yang. Shake things up."

She pushed herself up off the couch. "Which is why I'm going with you."

He stood as well, towering over her, purposely using his

size to try to intimidate. "You're staying here. That's my final decision."

She put her hands on her hips. "If you think you'll be able to walk out that door without me hot on your trail, *¡estás loco*!"

"Are you calling me *crazy*?"

"That's one interpretation, *gringo*."

He threw up his hands. "Fine. You win. You can come with me. But only if you follow rule number three."

"*Another* rule? How many are there?"

"I told you, I'm—"

"Making them up as you go, *sí, sí. Comprendo*. I understand. Just tell me this latest Beauism and let's get it over with."

She was so outrageous it made him want to laugh. He had to struggle to maintain his serious demeanor. This *was* serious. He needed her safe and preferred that she not go with him. But she did have a point. She was the yin to his yang. Or rather, she had a different perspective than he did because of her background being the opposite of his. As he interviewed people and tried to uncover information about her brother's comings and goings in Mystic Lake, her knowledge of her family and who they associated with could come in handy. Something he wouldn't think was useful might end up being a key to the investigation depending on her interpretation of it.

"The rule is that if you go with me, you do exactly what I say, when I say it."

"Control freak much?" she complained.

"I mean it, Sierra. Not because I want to boss you around. I don't get off on that, in case you haven't figured that out yet. I treat people with respect and expect the same in return. The reason I need you to follow my lead is to keep you safe. Period. I'm allowing you to go with me, not because of your threat but because it obviously is important to you. On the other hand, if you don't agree to rule number three, I'll handcuff you to the bed and go without you. Your choice."

She narrowed her eyes. "You wouldn't dare."

"Try me."

Her cheeks flushed. She was obviously on the verge of letting loose with one of her tirades. And while he secretly enjoyed the anticipation of finding out what outrageous things she would say every time she lost her temper, he didn't have time for it right now.

"Choose," he repeated. "If we leave now, we'll have a good six or seven hours of daylight. That may sound like a lot, but since we arrived by boat to avoid being seen by your brother and his men out on the roads, our only transportation right now is a combination of boating and hiking. Even using some of the tunnels around here as shortcuts, that will take a big chunk of our time just getting around. And when we do go out in the open, it will only be after carefully waiting and watching to ensure that your brother and his men aren't around. We need to leave now. I gave you your two options. Choose."

"Okay, okay. I agree to rule number three."

"And you'll still comply with my earlier rules."

"Yes, yes. I already said that."

"Then, let's go." He started toward the door.

"Wait."

He sighed and turned around. "What now?"

"I need my shoes. And I have to pee." She ran down the hallway, slamming the bathroom door behind her.

Beau blinked, then started laughing. He laughed so hard that Sierra started swearing at him in Spanish through the bathroom door. He hadn't missed her latest adorable tirade after all.

Chapter Fifteen

Sierra wanted so much to sit in the prow of the little fishing boat and watch the thick deep green forests rolling past. This was her first time on a boat in years, and she wanted to enjoy the beauty around her. But Beau insisted that she stay inside the small enclosure with him as he steered the boat. The tinted glass would help conceal their identities. That would make sense except that they hadn't passed any other boats, let alone seen any people on the banks, since they'd left the cabin half an hour earlier.

"Where is everyone?" she asked. "It's summer. I thought there would be lots of other boats. Tourists."

"This part of the river isn't that deep, and it's too narrow for a tourist or even a local to let loose on a speedboat without worrying about running aground. It'll open up soon, get much deeper and wider. That's when you'll see more boats."

She stood on her tiptoes, trying to peer through the glass down at the water. "How deep is it right now?"

He looked at a cluster of instruments. "Twenty feet, give or take."

"I'd think that was plenty deep for a speed boat."

"In a different section of the lake, I'd agree with you. But unless you're familiar with the hazards underneath the water, it would be foolish to do more than what we're doing."

"Going as slow as turtles?"

He laughed. "Not quite that slow. This past spring we had some torrential rains for several weeks. The river that comes down the mountain, feeding the lake, stirred everything up, moved hazards around. I haven't been out here since then. I'm being extra careful in case some of the debris under the water has shifted. The locals are well aware of what can happen around here. Tourists aren't. But they're warned at the boat ramps and the marina. This year, part of that warning is to steer clear of this section for now until it's fully investigated. That takes time and money the town doesn't always have in its budget."

She leaned against one of the windows again. "I know that people have died on this lake. How many have died this year so far?" When he didn't answer, she turned around.

His jaw was clenched as he carefully steered toward the middle of this section of the lake. "Too many," he finally answered. "Normally, midsummer, we might have had one, maybe two disappearances or proven deaths. But in the beginning of this year a family of five from Chattanooga came to try out their new boat, even though it was wicked cold and not the usual time for being on the water. They wanted to get used to the boat before summer and figured the cold months would be good for that since there wouldn't be many other boats around. In spite of the warnings at the marina, and the maps that Billy gave them of the known hazards—"

"Billy?"

"Bobby, actually. Bobby Thompson. But I've heard the kids around here tease him so much calling him Billy Bob that I sometimes slip up myself. He's the owner of the local marina, the guy who flies our medevac helicopter I told you about."

"Oh, right. I met Mr. Thompson when I was trying to get the names of my brother's friends. Why call him Billy Bob if his name is Bobby?"

"Billy Bob Thornton, the actor. Bobby looks a lot like him."

"Ah. Okay. So he warned this family and what happened? They ignored him?"

"I don't know if they purposely ignored him or got excited and forgot his warnings once they were out on the water without anyone else around to get in their way. They were in one of the hazardous areas they should have avoided and going way too fast. The hull of their boat hit the top of a tree that was hidden under the water. Peeled the boat apart like a can opener. Threw everyone into the water." He drew a deep breath and shook his head. "The family had life jackets on at the marina. For whatever reason, comfort or something else, they took them off once they were out of Bobby's sight. None of them survived." He tapped both of their life vests that they had on. "You never know when an accident is going to happen. That's why I insisted on these today."

She nodded, but it wasn't the vests she was thinking about. It was the mixture of frustration and sadness in Beau's expression that had her putting her hand on his on the wheel.

He tensed at her touch but didn't pull away.

"You really do take every death personally, don't you?" she said.

"Of course. My job is to—was to keep people safe, whether they live here or are tourists. Every preventable death is a failure we have to learn from, to try to prevent the next one. But when people don't listen…" He shook his head again. "It's… frustrating is all."

She dropped her hand to her side. "It is beautiful here, so much wilder than I'd expected. You'd think there would be cabins all along the shores. Water views like this are usually in high demand in other places. Why am I not seeing any here?"

"Do you always ask this many questions?"

"When I've got nothing else to do. Are you going to answer me?"

He turned the wheel slightly, steering the boat farther out toward the middle again. The current must have been pushing them toward shore because he kept having to make corrections in their course.

"Water views cost a pretty penny here in Mystic Lake too, but only in areas that aren't known to be full of underwater hazards. Because of how this lake was formed, the debris beneath the surface is substantial in most of it. That's actually one way to know you might be in a dangerous area out here. If you don't see cabins or docks, take that as a sign to be cautious of underwater debris. Another reason you don't see as many homes out here is that the lake is landlocked. In spite of how enormous it is, spanning for miles through the mountains, the only way to get to it is from our town. As you well know, that's an hour-long drive from the outskirts of Chattanooga. One way in, one way out. Unless you fly by helicopter. It can make people feel closed off, isolated."

He shrugged. "People who come here either love it or hate it, as far as actually living here goes. Personally, I'm glad that most of the visitors are temporary and don't choose to stay long-term. I like living in a small town and not having glass office buildings and concrete everywhere you look."

He glanced at her, his brows raising when he saw her looking at him. "Am I talking too much now?"

"It's nice. What else can you tell me about this place?"

"Enough to put you to sleep with boredom. Is there something specific you want to know?"

"Actually, there is. I've never been on the water here before, in spite of all the time I've spent in town. Would you show me where Esteban was supposedly killed? I was told that his body, or whoever's body was actually recovered, wasn't far from where he went into the water. But the company my family hired had been searching that area for months without finding anything. There had been a storm right before they supposedly found him, and they said it must have done what you said earlier, moved debris around. Including the skeletal remains they pulled out." She swallowed. "Remains I thought were my brother's for a very long time."

Beau moved some gears and the sound of the engines cut out. Then a metallic grinding noise sounded from the back of the boat. A slight jerk had her grabbing his arm to keep from falling.

"Sorry about that," he said, steadying her. "I should have warned you. I dropped anchor. This was actually my first planned destination today. We're already here, where Jake Randolph, aka your brother, allegedly went overboard."

She looked out the windows on all sides. "Doesn't look like a spot that's dangerous."

"Most of the dangerous places around here don't. Do you see any cabins or docks?"

She shook her head. "No. Just trees and muddy banks."

"This is one of the most dangerous parts of Mystic Lake. There's debris throughout this section. But there's something very interesting about where we are right now. I'll show you why." He stepped the few feet to the open doorway.

"I thought we weren't allowed out where someone could see us."

"We'll have to take some risks today or we won't get any information. I don't see anyone around and can't think of any reason for them to be. It seems safe. But if you're worried and don't want to—"

"No, I do. If you think it's safe, that's all I need to hear."

They headed out to the fishing area of the boat in the back, the only place that comfortably allowed them to move around because the boat was so small.

"Sit here," he said, guiding her to one of the built-in seating areas along one side. "The accident report listed the GPS location from the boat that Jake Randolph and his friends rented right around here."

"You memorized the GPS coordinates?"

"No, although I've been in this precise location before and remember it pretty well. I programmed the coordinates from Randolph's file into the boat's GPS tracker before we left our dock. His file is one of the ones that I put in my backpack at the station, before we headed down the road toward Chattanooga."

"Plan A."

"Yes, the infamous, ill-fated plan A. With plan B being a bust too, I'm hoping plan C will go far better."

"Plan C? Us, out here trolling for information?"

"Trolling. Yeah, I suppose that's exactly what we're doing. We're going to talk to a lot of people today, people I trust, like Bobby. Hopefully some of them will remember something about Randolph, or saw your father's men out here searching for his body or, more importantly, have seen your brother or his men out here in the past few weeks. If there are enough confirmed sightings we might be able to piece the information together to form a picture that will tell us why he's here and what he's really up to."

"And your team, the officers, are doing the same in town."

"In town and in the mountains around town, exactly. Knock-and-talks. That the name of the game today."

"Knock-and-talks? Like, knocking on someone's door and talking to them?"

"Exactly. The goal is that timeline I mentioned. We'll pull together all the puzzle pieces this evening and see if they form a picture."

"Starting here, where Esteban—Jake, I mean, or whoever was really here—went overboard."

"Exactly. The investigation into Randolph's accident centered right here because this is the GPS location where the boat was stationary for the longest period of time. It makes sense that this would be where he went over and his alleged friends searched for him. Look over the side. Be careful, hold on. But don't worry about tipping the boat. In spite of its small size, it's heavy and secure. Look in the water and tell me what you see."

She frowned. "I won't be able to see anything. The water's too dark."

"When you look at it from the wheelhouse it seems that way. But is it really? Look over the side. Straight down." When she hesitated he said, "Trust me."

She rolled her eyes and held onto the side of the boat. "Okay, but this seems silly. I won't be able to—wait, what the heck? I can see all the way to the bottom."

"Not quite. It's far too deep for that in this section. But it's clear, as it is in much of the lake. It's an optical illusion that makes you think the water is dark, murky. Although, it is murky in some areas. But most of it's like it is here. The mountains and woods surrounding the lake and the debris under the water combine to make it look dark when you look out, like when your boat is skimming along. But if you stop, at least in this area, obviously you can see pretty far down."

He waved a hand. "I'll stop with the physics lessons. But tell me what you actually see here, where Randolph supposedly went overboard and drowned."

She peered down, carefully scanning what was beneath the water. "I don't understand. I don't… I don't see anything but clear water that goes on and on. Where's all of this dangerous debris you mentioned?" She straightened. "Wait, you said the town cleans up hazardous debris once they're aware of it and have the budget. Did they clean it up?"

"No."

She blinked. "But that doesn't make any sense. Why would he fall overboard here when there isn't any kind of hazard to cause him to fall? Was that a lie too? My brother didn't actually fall off the boat? His friends—or whoever they were—didn't try to kill him? Good grief, I don't know what to believe anymore."

"I've been asking myself those questions ever since the Jake Randolph disappearance. It's never made sense to me that there would have been any kind of accident in this exact spot. Thirty feet away, all around us, sure. Plenty of debris there. But right here? Nothing. Now, knowing that the person using the Randolph alias is your brother, and that he's alive and well, what do you think did or did not actually happen that day?"

"Well, I guess it was all made up. After all, he faked his death."

"And yet, skeletal remains were found out here, by the company your family hired."

"Yes. And of course we believed it was Esteban. I mean, the skeleton had his clothes, his wallet." She blinked. "No. Wait. That doesn't make sense either. Unless...his death was planned from the beginning. The other man, the one we buried. But that would mean Esteban killed him, used him to fake his death. No, no I don't believe he'd do that. Someone must have tried to kill Esteban. But he managed to swim away. Then, when my family kept searching for his body, he, what, took a corpse from a grave and dressed it like him to make us think it was him?"

Beau stared at her. "And you don't think you're a good investigator."

She shook her head. "I know I'm not. I'm just throwing

out potential scenarios and questions. I don't have any facts and have no idea if anything I'm saying is even feasible or makes sense."

"It is. It does. My point in bringing you out here is to show you that an accidental drowning doesn't pass the smell test, not to me. It didn't back then either, when it first happened, which is why we searched for weeks for Randolph's body. But given the history of this lake, after so much time passed, without any evidence to point to foul play we had to accept that he'd drowned and once again the lake refused to give up a body."

"Makes sense," she said. "I guess."

"Just theories. Things to think about."

He helped her up, and they headed back behind the glass.

They spent the rest of the day hunting pieces of the puzzle. First, they confirmed the path of her brother's boat—or the man who'd died in his place—recording what they'd found in an electronic notebook Beau had brought. Then they tied the boat to a tree that had fallen into the water along the shore, and Beau took her into some of the tunnels in the area to avoid the larger numbers of people they were starting to see out on the lake on docks they'd passed.

Once they'd emerged from the tunnels, he'd led her to the homes of people he knew well and trusted. Without telling them exactly who she was, other than his investigative assistant, he'd grilled them for information. Little by little they were hearing of more and more sightings of strangers in the area, men Beau and her both believed were working with her brother. And what seemed to be a few actual sightings of her brother as well. She didn't know what to make of these so-called puzzle pieces. But Beau dutifully recorded everything.

By the time they'd returned to their cabin, showered and devoured the frozen pepperoni pizza they'd baked in the cabin's oven, they were both exhausted. But at least they weren't hungry anymore.

As she plopped onto the couch to wait for Beau to set up his laptop with the TV again, she crossed her arms in frustration. Her tired brain didn't want to have another online meeting with his team to explore what they'd all found out today. And even though her body was just as tired as her mind, she'd have perked right up if given the opportunity to explore *Beau.*

Good grief, he was appealing. Smart and kind in spite of him being a cop. And fascinating and sexy and—okay, she was going in circles. She liked everything about him except for his former occupation. Well, that and those rules he was so fond of. And she really, really wanted to find out whether he felt the same heat that she felt every time they casually touched or looked into each other's eyes. Never in her life could she have imagined being so all-consumingly attracted to a police officer. Or to anyone, really. But Beau, well, he wasn't like anyone she'd ever met before.

What would her father do if she brought Beau home to meet him? He'd be horrified. Heck, he'd probably threaten to shoot him. But he was all bark and little bite as far as she was concerned. He'd come around eventually if she cared about Beau and he cared about her. Wouldn't he?

She bit her bottom lip, not nearly as certain as she'd like to be that her father would ever warm up to the idea of her dating a cop. And even though she loved and adored her father, she wasn't blind. She knew he wasn't exactly a law-abiding citizen. Okay, not at all a law-abiding citizen. Not as bad as the FBI believed him to be: she'd never think that. But she knew he was bad enough as far as bending and breaking laws that he'd probably go to prison for the rest of his life if he was ever convicted. Would Beau be safe in her world, if her father didn't agree to her seeing him? She was more than a little worried that she wouldn't like the honest answer to that question.

Maybe she'd never have to find out the answer. Beau was every bit the kind of man a woman in her position should avoid. Kind of the opposite of a bad boy. That must be why she practically drooled when she was around him. He was forbidden fruit. All she needed to do was take him to bed. Spend one incredibly hot, passionate night in his arms to get him out of her system. He wouldn't be so deliciously compelling after she'd crossed that line. He'd be like any other man. Well, not like any other man. Guys as buff, tall, deep-voiced and bedroom-eyed as Beau didn't come along very often. But they were out there. She'd just move on to one of them. One who wasn't in law enforcement. All would be right with her world again. Well, after they solved this investigation and—

"Sierra? Sierra? Can you hear me?"

She blinked and realized Beau was waving a hand in front of her face, his brow furrowed with concern. Over his shoulder she could see his officers on the TV ready for the status meeting. And they were looking at her too.

Her face heated. "Sorry. I, uh, kind of zoned out, I guess."

"You're really tired, aren't you? Do you want to go to bed and get some rest? I can handle the meeting without you if you prefer."

Resting was the last thing she wanted to do in bed tonight. She coughed and cleared her throat. "I, uh—no, thanks. I'd like to find out what's happening with the investigation."

He gave her a questioning look. "Are you sure you're okay?"

She swore in Spanish. "Can we get on with this?"

He grinned and sat back against the couch, facing the TV. "She's fine. Collier, this is your meeting. You want to start?"

Sierra scooted a little closer to Beau, smiling at his questioning look as if she didn't know why he'd glanced at her.

He nodded at something one of the officers was saying. She yawned and rubbed her eyes, then closed them to help relieve the burn. She really was tired.

The couch suddenly dipped, and some kind of cloth brushed lightly against her face. She swatted it away and opened her eyes. Except, she wasn't on the couch, she was on a bed. And Beau was holding the edge of the comforter, apparently trying to tuck her in.

"Hey, Sleeping Beauty. Sorry about the comforter. It slipped from my grip as I lowered you to the bed. Close your eyes and go back to sleep. I'll update you on things in the morning."

He stepped back and started to turn around.

"Wait." She sat up and grabbed his hand. "I fell asleep?"

"About five seconds after you closed your eyes in the meeting. You didn't miss much. We don't have any good leads yet on your brother. Go to sleep. We'll talk tomorrow."

She was in bed. Beau was here with her. Sleep? Heck no. She was wide awake now and ready to test her theory, to work him out of her system.

He tugged his hand to leave.

She tightened her grip.

"Sierra, is something wrong?"

"I just, uh..." She wiggled her toes. "You took off my shoes?"

"I did. Before you get outraged, that's all I took off. I didn't figure you'd want your shoes on in bed. Now, if you'll just let my hand go, I'll leave you—"

"Don't go." She threw the covers off and rose to her knees, taking his other hand and pulling him toward her. "Stay. Here. With me. It's a big bed. And I don't snore. Wait, do you snore?"

He chuckled. "Not that I've ever been told. I appreciate the offer of the bed, but the couch is quite comfortable. You don't have to share."

"I want to. Share." She stared up into his dark eyes, the dim light from the hallway just enough to highlight the masculine angles of his handsome face. "Everything. I want to share me."

His eyes widened. He slowly shook his head. "I think you must still be half-asleep, Sierra. I'm Beau Dawson. Police officer. Remember?"

"And I'm Sierra Covington, law-abiding daughter of a less-than-straight-and-narrow man, according to the FBI. If you can look past that, I can look past you being a cop."

He smiled. "Good to know. But, uh, even though I'm flattered by your…offer, I don't think this is the right time to—"

"Now is the perfect time." She tightened her hold on his hands and yanked as hard as she could.

Caught off guard, he tumbled forward, catching himself with his elbows to keep from crushing her. But the lower part of his body was plastered against her.

She wiggled beneath him.

He groaned.

"Don't try to deny what's incredibly, impressively obvious. You want me."

"Yeah, well. Don't take it personally. My body always reacts this way when a sleepy, gorgeous nymph offers everything and pulls me down on top of her."

"This happens a lot to you?" she teased.

"All the time. It's embarrassing, really. Always having to fight off beautiful women throwing themselves at me."

"Is that so?"

"Yep. Like I said, don't take it personally. We both need our sleep, and I really, really don't think that you'd want this if you were completely wide awake. You'll thank me in the morning." He rolled off her to the other side of the mattress.

Before he could get up, she pounced, straddling his hips and holding onto his shirt with a tight grip.

He grabbed her hands to stop her.

"Ouch," she said, pretending that he'd hurt her.

He immediately let go. "Sorry, did I—" His eyes narrowed. "You little minx. I didn't actually hurt you, did I? Let go of my shirt."

"Beau, please, wait. I want—"

He lifted her off him and set her down on the bed, then jumped to his feet.

"Tomorrow," he said. "We'll talk tomorrow. About the case, about this—I don't know—whatever is going on between us. People in forced proximity can think they're attracted to each other when, in the normal day-to-day world, that might never happen between them."

He headed for the door.

Sierra sat up again, wiping at the danged wetness running down her cheeks. "What is the real world, Beau? Is it yours? Or mine?"

He stopped, his arms gripping both sides of the doorframe, his back to her. Without turning around, he said, "Maybe a mixture of both." His voice was quiet, strained.

She closed her eyes and wiped at the humiliating tears.

The bed dipped.

Her eyes flew open to see Beau sitting beside her, his gaze searching hers. "Why are you crying?"

"Oh, heck if I know. I hate crying. I'm just… It's too much, you know? Everything going on. And this stupid attraction for you. It's like…lava, in my veins. Every single time we get close I burn. And it's not just tonight. It's not because I was tired and fell asleep on the couch. It's every dang minute since I saw your sweaty, incredible body chopping wood at your cabin. I knew you were a policeman then, and I still wanted you. I've wanted you ever since. And I thought, tonight, that maybe, just maybe, if we made love that would get you out of my system, you know? It's danged inconvenient feeling this way. Like you said, different worlds. I just wanted to—"

"Get me out of your system?"

"Exactly. I assure you the way I'm feeling isn't that forced proximity thing you mentioned. And I'm sure not sleepy. Not anymore. I know exactly what I'm doing." She wiped at her cheeks again. "*¡Ay, caramba!*"

"Here. Let me." He took the edge of his shirt and gently dried her tears. "Better?"

She let out a shaky breath. *"Sí. Gracias."* She made a shooing motion with her hand. "Go on. I'm embarrassed enough throwing myself at a man who doesn't want me. Not with his mind anyway, even if his body has other ideas."

He laughed and shook his head. "You really are something."

"So I've been told. Go."

He gently ran a finger down the side of her face. "I'll go. If that's what you want."

She grew still. "And if it's not what I want?"

"You're wide awake?"

"Yes."

"You really want to work me out of your system?"

"Boy, do I."

He laughed. "Not the most flattering reaction I've ever heard." His smile faded, and his expression turned serious, tense. "But it's better than I ever hoped to get from one of the most interesting, smart and fascinating women I've ever met."

He pulled her onto his lap and kissed her. It wasn't a soft, questioning kiss. It wasn't tender or hesitant in any way. It was ravenous, consuming and so hot she was whimpering with pleasure and practically climbing him to get closer. When they finally broke apart, they were both panting, hearts racing, staring at each other in wonder.

"Wow," she breathed.

He grinned.

"I hope you're ready for a long night," she whispered. "I think it might take quite a while to work through this inconvenient attraction of ours."

"Sadly, kissing is all we can do. It didn't occur to me to bring protection on this trip."

"I noticed there was a, um, box in the top drawer of the nightstand. The cabin owner must have left it there."

He blinked. "Are you kidding?"

"Nope."

He leaned past her and got the box. A moment later, he pressed a soft kiss against her lips. "You're sure you want this?"

"I need this. I need you, Beau. Please. Love me."

"Whatever the beautiful lady wants." He pulled her in for another steamy kiss and pressed her back against the mattress.

A LONG TIME LATER, she woke up in his arms, blinking up at the dimly lit ceiling. Beau Dawson was the stuff of dreams. He'd satisfied her in ways she'd never thought possible, and yet, here she was, burning for him all over again. She drummed her short nails on the mattress. Tried counting sheep. Recited the alphabet both forward and backward in her mind, trying not to feel this way.

It was no use.

"Beau?" she whispered. "Are you awake?" She lightly pressed his shoulder. "Beau? Are you sleeping?"

"Not anymore," he grumbled.

"It didn't work."

He chuckled. "I beg to disagree. It worked quite well. Twice."

"That's not what I meant."

He turned on his side facing her in all his glory. "Still feeling attracted to a washed-up former police chief?"

"Unfortunately."

"We need some sleep if we're going to function in the morning."

"Then, make it quick. Hurry."

He was laughing as he covered her body with his.

Chapter Sixteen

When Beau woke up the next morning, he immediately realized his world had changed forever. The incredible night he'd spent with the delightfully sassy woman still sleeping beside him had left him sore and tired. But it had also left a mark on his heart, maybe even his soul. He'd fallen for her, hard. And he hadn't even known it, not until she'd shed those heartbreaking tears and asked him to help her get him out of her system. She was now entrenched in his. And he didn't even feel guilty about it.

As a lifelong law enforcement officer, he knew the risks, knew the payment that this night would require. He'd never be able to go back into law enforcement again, not after having a relationship with the daughter of an organized crime boss. No reputable agency would want him within a mile of them. It didn't matter that Sierra was innocent, not caught up in that life of crime. It was guilt by association—her because of her family, Beau because of Sierra.

And he didn't care.

At least, not now. Not yet. It would come, eventually. The regret about destroying his career. All he'd ever wanted in his professional life was to help others, get criminals off the streets. That deep yearning for that life would come back. It had been ingrained in him too long not to. But he instinctively knew it still wouldn't matter. Trading Sierra for a career wasn't an option. Not for him. He would eventually grieve for what he'd lost. But he'd rejoice over what he'd found.

Sierra.

That is, if she wanted him in her life. That was the worry that had him lying there so long, watching her, waiting for her to open her eyes. He needed to know how she felt now that their wild night was over. Would she regret it, in spite of insisting that it was what she'd wanted? Would she be relieved that she had, indeed, gotten over him? Not knowing was killing him. If it was simply a one-night fling for her, he'd have to figure out how to pretend that was okay.

He silently swore. When had he become a dramatic, melancholy love-sick fool? This was ridiculous. He had work to do, a mystery to solve, a woman to protect. He'd never been this sappy in his life, and he damn well wasn't going to start now.

He flipped back the covers and swung his legs over the side of the bed. He'd made it to the bathroom door, when an irritated voice called out behind him.

"Where do you think you're going?"

He looked over his shoulder, his mouth watering at the sight of the disheveled naked beauty sitting up in bed glaring at him.

"I need a shower," he said, barely able to force the words through his tight throat. Good grief, she was beautiful. Her long dark hair cascaded down her body in glorious disarray, a soft curl teasing him as it dangled over one breast.

"So do I." She crawled out of bed and padded across the carpet to stop in front of him. "Or do you prefer to shower alone?" She ran her tongue across his chest, then leaned against him, her soft curves crushed against his stomach. "Well?"

He groaned as his body jumped painfully to attention.

She grinned.

"Does this mean last night didn't work?" he asked, the love-sick puppy inside him holding its breath waiting for her reply.

"Not even a little bit. Guess we'll have to try again." She grabbed his hand and tugged him into the bathroom.

IT HAD BEEN another long day for the two of them, but this time Beau had kept Sierra in the cabin. They hadn't risked going out again because Officers O'Brien and Fletcher had documented no fewer than five sightings yesterday by witnesses who believe they'd seen someone matching Esteban's description. If it truly was her brother they'd seen, then he'd kept to the outskirts of town, away from the more populated parts of Mystic Lake. And he was definitely searching for something. Or someone. That was enough for Beau to decide his primary duty today was as Sierra's bodyguard. He was leaving the knock-and-talks to his former team.

Time passed quickly. Their relationship was fresh, new. They both wanted to know everything they could about each other. Of course, he already knew a lot about her family, having read many law enforcement briefs and bulletins about them over the years. And she'd studied up on him online and learned more by planting those cameras—which he'd forgotten to follow up on—in the police station and the mayor's office. She wasn't perfect. No one was. But she wasn't her father either, not even close.

She shared the personal side to the statistics and facts he knew about her family. Like that her mother had passed away a year before Esteban had allegedly died, and how hard both of their losses were on the family. Her mother had been diagnosed with breast cancer. She was determined to fight it, then when the treatments weren't going well, she'd decided to take her own life. She'd overdosed on pain pills and had been found by Sierra's father.

"He was devastated, of course," she said. "We all were. I still don't understand why my mom did that. But I haven't been in her situation either. If I was in all of that pain, feeling miserable every day, maybe I'd give up too."

He'd hugged her and offered what comfort he could. But in the face of a loss like that, he felt completely inadequate. One thing was clear: she'd worshiped her mother and adored her father. And she felt the same way about her brothers, both biological and step. Even knowing that Esteban might be her enemy now, until she understood why, she couldn't quite accept it. It was obvious that part of her desperately hoped there was another explanation.

When it was her turn to ask questions, she'd wanted to know about his family and what he'd been like as a child. He told her some of the details about his rather average life. A schoolteacher mom. A father who was an engineer. He had three younger brothers.

"An engineer? And you lived here, in Mystic Lake? Where did he work?"

"Chattanooga. Lots of people here work there since our only real industry is tourism. Long drive, a little over an hour and a half each way because of it being across town. When I was in middle school and my brothers were starting elementary school, he and my mom both got jobs in Florida, down near Tampa where some of our distant relatives live."

"That's quite the move. How did you end up back here?"

"I never left. I pitched a fit, ran away. Dad tanned my hide when he found me and brought me home. But I ran away again. I was a brat, not wanting to leave my friends. My dad pretty much gave up in disgust. Mom worked out an agreement with some close family friends to let me stay with them until I graduated high school. Remember me telling you about the chicken farmers not far from the safe house?"

"No way. Is that where you ended up? At their farm?"

"No. I lived on a horse ranch, in a valley at about the farthest corner of the mountains where you can go without leaving the official Mystic Lake town limits. But those nice people I still owe egg money to are distant cousins of the family who took me in."

"Small town."

"Small town," he agreed. "That's pretty much my story. I went to college after high school, never moved to Florida. I see my family at Christmas every year, when my brothers fly in from where they've moved and started their own families. That's our annual reunion, more or less."

"You only see each other once a year? But you're family."

"Without much in common, little to talk about."

"That's sad," she said. "I can't imagine not seeing or at least talking to my family on a regular basis." She grimaced. "Then again, it's been a ridiculously long time since I've seen, or at least really spoken to Esteban. The jerk. Pretending he was dead."

She'd gone on to fuss and cuss about her brother, as Beau would expect. They'd discussed other things, details about the investigation too. But what she never mentioned was any regret over spending last night with him—or this morning. There was no awkwardness between them. And the hungry looks she gave him off and on had him wanting to take her back to bed. But with so much unresolved around the shootings, and neither of them wanting to have to hide out the rest of their lives, they were determined to be proactive. They agreed that they needed to focus on trying to solve the mysteries surrounding her brother.

To that end, they sat at the kitchen table for hours, reviewing information they and the officers had gathered the day before. They only got up for bathroom breaks and food. Then they would come right back to the table to pour over reports and old files on other disappearances in case there were any similarities.

There weren't.

He sat back and stretched. "When I briefed you earlier today on the status meeting you missed, there's one thing I forgot to mention. There's evidence the tunnel that we used to get to the safe house was how Esteban and his men found us. They had cut away the vines and bushes that camouflaged the entrance. Shoeprints in the tunnel matched ones found outside the safe house, prints that were in addition to yours and mine."

Her eyes widened. "Do you think they found it because I used that burner phone to talk to Rafael? They somehow traced a call in the area and it helped them find the tunnel?"

"Tracing the call wouldn't have helped them discover the tunnel entrance. It would have only gotten them to the general area of this mountain. Did you mention anything to Rafael about the tunnel?"

She briefly closed her eyes as if in pain. "You asked me that once before and I didn't think I had. But I've replayed that phone conversation with Rafael in my head plenty of times since then. I think I did mention the tunnel, kind of as an aside. Nothing specific. It's not like I gave him the location. Even if I wanted to, I couldn't have explained right where it was. All I did was brief him about the shooting at your cabin, then us being shot at on the road and having to head up the mountain and use a tunnel to get to safety. But that wouldn't have mattered unless he called Esteban after that." She blinked, her eyes widening. "No. No, he wouldn't have. Couldn't have. He didn't even know Esteban was alive until I told him. Esteban's old phone number is out of service. Rafael wouldn't have any way of contacting him."

Beau sat back. "I think you just fit some puzzle pieces together for us. I'll bet that's exactly what happened. Rafael called Esteban and told him what you said, and Esteban used that information to search the mountain and then used the tunnel. At some point, since faking his death, Esteban has reached out to your other brother and they've kept in touch."

She crossed her arms. "That sounds like unsubstantiated theories and conjecture to me. Isn't it possible that Rafael has had no contact with Esteban and has nothing to do with him finding us at that first cabin? Maybe Esteban just kept searching the mountain trying to find us and stumbled onto the entrance to the tunnel."

"Anything's possible," he conceded.

"I can tell by your tone that you don't believe that's what happened, do you?"

"It seems unlikely. I don't think someone finding the opening to a dark, incredibly long tunnel in the mountain would want to venture inside without being positive it wouldn't collapse and would lead them somewhere useful. It's far more reasonable to conclude that either Rafael helped Esteban fake his death and stay out of sight all this time, or Esteban contacted him later for his help. Now one of them, maybe both, are trying to find you. The question is why, and do they want to harm you? The shootings definitely have me leaning toward the latter."

"None of this makes sense to me."

"Go back to the beginning. Everything that's happened seems to stem from Esteban being on that boat and disappearing. That's probably the key to figuring this out. Maybe we haven't gotten traction with our theories because our initial premise is wrong. What if Esteban was never on the boat? Maybe he came here specifically to stage his death, then brought the skeletal remains of someone else's corpse months later and sank them in the lake to try to get people to stop looking for him. Your family didn't perform DNA testing on the remains, right?"

She shook her head. "No. The clothing, his phone, wallet, the gold chain he wore around his neck were all with the skeleton. We had no reason not to think it was him."

"He must have placed those items there to make you think it was him."

She considered that. "You're saying he went there knowing that someone was trying to kill him? And that he planned out the boat scenario to make them think he died?"

"It's feasible. Plausible even, given what we do and don't know about the boat and situation back then."

"I can see him doing that if he felt he had no other choice. If he made a powerful enemy, though, and knew his life was in danger, why not go to my father for help? It's not like my father couldn't step in. He's powerful, with significant resources. He could have protected Esteban. So why didn't Esteban go to him?"

He stared at her. "Congratulations, Sierra. I think you just put everything together. It's so obvious that it never occurred to me. Esteban faked his death because he knew he was in danger and needed to disappear, permanently. He had to disappear because the one person who could help him was the one trying to kill him."

"No. No, Beau. Don't you dare go there." Sierra held out her hands as if to stop his next words.

"Your father. He's the one trying to kill your brother. That's why Esteban has surrounded himself with gunmen. They're his bodyguards. But they're getting too zealous in their efforts to protect him. Either that, or it's on purpose and—"

"Stop it. Just stop. My father wouldn't try to kill my brother. And Esteban isn't trying to kill me. You, maybe. Yes. I admit that if he doesn't want you digging into the cold case and proving he's alive, he would…he might…do something about you. To stop you. But he wouldn't need to kill me. There's no motive. No reason. No advantage."

She stood and paced back and forth in the small kitchen area, her hair bouncing around her shoulders. "And you don't know my father. All you know is what you've read in those impersonal police reports. He wouldn't hurt any of us. He couldn't. He loves us. We're not like your family. We actually care about each other."

"Ouch. Guess I deserved that."

She stopped pacing, her expression filled with regret. "I'm sorry. That was awful." She crossed to him and leaned down, hugging him. "I shouldn't have said that. Our families are different. That doesn't mean yours love each other any less than mine."

He pulled her arms down from his neck and stood, pulling her against him and resting his cheek against the top of her head. "Stop apologizing. It was nothing."

Her arms tightened, and she buried her face against his chest. It was then that he realized her reaction wasn't just about the little zinger she'd thrown at him about his family. It was about her realizing that *her* family might not be as close and strong as she'd always believed. Even the idea that her father could be the bad guy in this situation hurt her. Beau silently chastised himself for being so callous in tossing around his theories. He should have saved those for his team.

"Let's drop that line of thought for now." He rubbed his hand gently up and down her back. "I'm probably wrong anyway. Heck, we don't even have to discuss the investigation. We can wait until the team status call later to see what they've come up with."

She sniffed, obviously trying to hold back tears. Damn. He really should have kept his mouth shut. She was so strong, and smart and fun to brainstorm with that he'd forgotten how soft-hearted she could be. Like when she'd worked so hard to save the gunman who was bleeding to death on the road after the same man had just tried to kill the two of them. Most people wouldn't have done that.

"Come on," he said. "Let's take a break. Maybe watch a movie in a bit. I can pop a mean bowl of popcorn, assuming this cabin has some." He scooped her up against his chest and carried her to the couch where he sat with her on his lap.

He held her tight, lightly rocking her and playing with the incredibly soft curls hanging down her back. She settled more closely, her curves fitting perfectly against his planes. He held her tight, full of wonder that she still trusted him to hold her and soothe her in spite of the hurt being his fault.

Then he heard it. An odd little catch in her breath. Then another. This time louder. He grinned. She *did* snore.

Chapter Seventeen

Sierra idly moved her pretzels on her plate, forming a carbohydrate moat around her grilled cheese sandwich.

Beau set his spoon in his now-empty bowl of tomato soup and slid it across the kitchen table out of the way. "You told me you loved grilled cheese. You haven't eaten a single bite."

"I ate the soup. It was good. Thanks."

He shook his head. "I can open a can and heat it with the best of them. What's wrong?"

"Other than the obvious? Someone wants to kill us and it may or may not be my own brother? Oh, wait, and my father may be trying to kill him?"

"Guess I deserved that. I should have asked what *else* is wrong? Are you getting sick?"

"More like I've lost my appetite because I'm feeling guilty. My formerly dead brother is very much alive and I haven't really thought about whoever is buried in his grave. I can only hope, pray, he truly was dug up and his skeleton used by my brother as opposed to my brother…hurting him."

She pushed her plate back and straightened in her chair. "We need to find out who's buried in the Covington family cemetery and notify *his* family. To them, he's either…missing…or he died a long time ago and his true grave is empty. Either way, they deserve to know what happened, or at least, where he is so they can give him a proper burial in his own plot of land with his own tombstone."

"I agree. Which is why I asked Collier last night to get paperwork ready so that once we have tangible evidence to prove the body isn't Esteban's, we can get a court order to perform an exhumation. He's also searching for missing persons reports in neighboring counties around the time your brother's alleged remains were found to try to narrow down potential identities for our John Doe. Where is your family cemetery? That address will be needed for Collier's paperwork."

"On the acreage behind the Covington mansion outside of Memphis. Pretty much a direct walk from our back door. But it's a long walk."

"Huge back yard I take it?"

"Reminiscent of Central Park. It's quite beautiful."

"I'm sure it is. I'll let Collier know when we're online in a few more hours."

"Do you think they've found my brother yet?"

"Doubtful. If they had, they'd have been knocking on our door to let us know."

A knock sounded at the door.

They both looked at each other in surprise, then shoved out of their chairs.

Beau pulled out his gun. "While that could be Collier or the others," he said, keeping his voice low so no one outside would hear him, "until I know for sure, stay out of sight. Go to the bedroom and wait there."

He moved to the window to the left of the door in the kitchen area and peered out the blinds. He swore when he saw who it was.

The sound of the door creaking had him jumping back just as Sierra swung it open.

"Esteban!" she cried out.

Beau grabbed Sierra's waist and yanked her away from her brother.

Esteban stepped inside just as Beau was whirling back toward him. He dove at Esteban, tackling him to the floor and shoving his right arm up between his shoulder blades.

"Don't move," Beau growled, pressing the bore of his pistol against the other man's temple.

"Beau, stop it," Sierra cried out. "He's unarmed."

"Which is the only reason I didn't shoot him. Yet. Stop squirming, Covington."

"You're breaking my damn arm, cop."

Beau eased his arm down a fraction. "Better?"

Esteban glared at him, his cheek plastered against the hardwood floor. "A little," he gritted out.

"Sierra," Beau said, not taking his eyes off her brother, "get my handcuffs. They're in the nightstand, my side of the bed."

Esteban's eyes widened. "*Your* side of the bed? You bastard."

"Oh, now you're worried about your little sister. After making me think you were dead all this time!"

"You don't understand." Her brother jerked against Beau's hold and tried to get up. Beau shoved his arm higher again.

Esteban let loose with a string of curse words, half in English and half in Spanish.

Sierra ran out of the room. When she returned, she gave Beau the handcuffs.

As soon as he had them on his prisoner, he jerked Esteban to his feet and holstered his pistol. Then he proceeded to pat Esteban down, checking for weapons.

"I'm unarmed, *cop*," he practically spat out.

"*Cop* sounds far less insulting coming from your sister." Beau forced him to sit on the couch, facing him.

"I knew you were trouble," Esteban said. He looked at Sierra standing beside Beau. "And you. Screwing a police chief? What were you thinking?"

"Watch your mouth," Beau growled. "Treat her with respect. Anything happening between her and me is our business, not yours."

"My sister is definitely my business. Keep your hands off her or answer to me."

"Shut up, Esteban," Sierra told him.

She stepped closer to Beau's side, surprising him with her show of support.

Her brother aimed a hurt look at her. "You have no idea what I've been through, what I've risked to come here. And you're taking his side? Have you no loyalty anymore?"

She rolled her eyes. "Loyal to who? You're dead. Right?"

"I know, I know. I put you through a lot by letting you think I'd drowned. But I had no choice. I was trying to protect you."

She sighed and started toward him. Beau grabbed her hand and tugged her to the other couch that formed an *L* with the first one.

"You can let go of her now," Esteban bit out.

Beau let go, then settled his arm around her shoulders.

Esteban narrowed his eyes.

Beau smiled.

Sierra pushed Beau's arm off her. "Enough. Stop it, you two. Esteban, you said you went through a lot to come here and what you did was to protect me. Explain. Tell us what the heck is going on and why in the world you let your family believe you were dead."

A loud, rapid knock sounded on the door.

"Who the hell's here now?" Beau stood, then hesitated. "Sierra—"

"I know. I know. Don't trust my brother." She pulled her pistol out of her ankle holster.

Beau blinked. "I thought I took that away after the safe house. How long have you had it? I didn't see it last night when I took off your shoes."

"I'll kill you!" Esteban said.

"Shut up," Sierra and Beau both told him.

He mumbled something under his breath.

"I took it when I got the handcuffs," Sierra said. "I wanted to make sure I could protect you if my brother was a jerk."

"Sierra!" Esteban complained. When they both turned toward him, he said, "I know, I know. Shut up."

"Be careful," Beau reminded Sierra. "Remember rule number two. Heck, rule number one as well, depending on who's at the door. For that matter, number three. I told you to go to the bedroom, not open the door earlier."

"You're getting far too bossy."

"What are all these rules?" her brother asked.

"Shut up," they both said again.

"Stay here, Sierra," Beau said. "I mean it."

"I've got this." She pointed her gun at the floor, her gaze locked on Esteban.

He gave her a bewildered look.

The loud knock sounded again. "Open up," a man called out. "It's Rafael. I know my brother and sister are in there."

Beau stopped in surprise at the door and slowly turned to look at Sierra and her brother. "Rafael? What is this, a family reunion?"

She lifted her shoulders in a helpless gesture. "I have no idea what's going on."

Esteban swore.

"For once, I agree with you," Beau told him.

He aimed his pistol at the door and jerked it open.

The dark-haired man standing there raised his hands in the air. "I left my gun on the porch, over there. I'm unarmed."

"You don't mind if I verify that, do you? Turn around."

"Um. Sure." Rafael turned around, and Beau roughly patted him down.

When Beau stepped back, he motioned Rafael to come inside. "Welcome to our humble abode, Covington. I'll get the beer and chips," he said, sarcasm dripping from every word. He yanked the confused-looking man across the threshold and slammed the door behind him.

Chapter Eighteen

Sierra tapped her foot impatiently, sitting beside Beau on the couch. It no longer formed an *L* with the other couch. Instead, Beau had scooted it under the TV, at least fifteen feet away from her brothers, facing them. To top that off, since he didn't have another set of handcuffs, he'd had the audacity to tie Rafael's hands behind him using a cord that Beau had cut from a lamp. She supposed he'd have to pay for that too once this was all over, along with the pilfered eggs.

Worst of all, he'd taken her gun away. That had her madder than anything else. It meant he didn't trust her. He'd said as much when he'd chided her for breaking rule number three—or was it two? The one where she had to mind him at all times during the investigation. She couldn't help it if her excitement at seeing her brother had her opening the door. Although, to Beau's credit, she'd have never known her brother was outside if she'd gone to the bedroom when Beau told her to instead of looking out the living room window.

Ugh. He was infuriating. And her hero as well, dang it. Because everything he was doing that aggravated her was to keep her safe. It was hard maintaining her anger while secretly being grateful and in awe of him at the same time.

She glanced at him, speaking on his phone to Collier, and arched a brow. "Can we move this along? I want to talk to my brothers."

"Just a minute," he promised her. "Collier, one more thing. Is Fletcher there with you? She is? Good. I'm about to interrogate the Covington brothers—"

Esteban swore at him in Spanish.

"—and as you can probably already hear, I'm guessing they may try to use Spanish to keep me from knowing everything they discuss. I'd like Fletcher to interpret if that happens. Yes, I'll put it on Speaker mode." He pressed a button on the phone and set it on the coffee table he'd moved to the middle of the floor between the couches for just that reason. Then he sat beside Sierra.

"I'll start," Beau said.

"They're my brothers. I'll start."

"This is an interrogation, Sierra. Not a family reunion. Remember—"

"Don't you dare mention one of your rules again. Fine. I'll wait. But don't expect me to remain silent if I want clarification about anything."

"Thanks, sweetheart." He winked when Esteban mumbled beneath his breath, his eyes narrowed dangerously.

"Stop antagonizing him," she chided.

"What's going on?" Rafael asked. "I think I missed something."

Esteban nodded toward Beau. "That cop and our sister are…" he hesitated when Beau gave him a sharp look, "… *dating*."

Rafael's mouth dropped open. "Sierra, you're dating a *cop*?"

She threw her hands up. "Good grief. Can we just move on? Beau, ask your questions or I'm going to."

"Do either of you have anyone outside? If you do, just know that police officer Fletcher and her team will be here in minutes if things go bad. And she can have the sheriff's office block the main road and send reinforcements."

Esteban let loose with a litany of Spanish.

Sierra was exceedingly grateful that Beau couldn't understand all the rude insults her brother was spewing.

Fletcher spoke through the speaker. "That means—"

"I know what that means," Beau said. "Or the gist of it. No need to interpret." He looked from Esteban to Rafael. "Do you have any backup outside? I don't want a repeat of Sierra being caught in the middle of gunfire again because of some stupid stunt that one of you pulls. If shots are fired anywhere near her, I'll put a bullet in both of you. Understood?"

Sierra stiffened beside him but remained silent. She wasn't sure whether he was serious or not. But she was trying hard to trust him, in spite of his apparent doubts about her.

Rafael immediately shook his head. "I came here alone. I didn't tell anyone I was coming. Except Esteban. He called me a little over an hour ago. Sierra had already told me he was alive. So it wasn't as big a shock as it would have been. I was out of town, out of state when she called, so it took a while to get here. I'd just landed at the Chattanooga airport when Esteban called and said to meet him and Sierra here."

"Esteban, how did you know she was here, in this cabin?" Beau asked.

Esteban gave him a surly expression and didn't answer.

Sierra went off in Spanish at him, basically telling him to man up and take responsibility for his actions.

His expression turned sheepish, like a child who'd just been scolded.

"Did you want that interpreted?" Fletcher asked through the speaker.

"I'll do it," Sierra said. "I called him an idiot and told him to answer the questions."

"Close enough." There was laughter in Fletcher's voice. "That's the G-rated version."

Beau smiled. “Esteban.” This time his voice was a little less impatient, a little less gruff. “Your anger at me is quite convincing. Either you’re a great actor, or you really are upset on your sister’s behalf. Understand where I’m coming from, though. She’s nearly been killed several times this week. You always seem to be involved in those incidents. Are you trying to have her killed, or is there another explanation?”

Rafael stared at his brother. “What the heck, Esteban? You’re behind the shootings she told me about?”

Esteban’s face took on a pained expression. “I trusted the wrong people. Idiots. Okay? That’s all. I was on the run and had to hire my own mercenary muscle for protection. I knew better. People who hire out to the highest bidder have no loyalties. When things get rough, it’s every man for himself and they don’t care who gets in the way. The ones Dawson didn’t kill were fired. I let go of every single one of them.”

“What about that Randy guy?” Sierra asked. “The one you gave the transfusion. Your friend.”

He rolled his eyes. “He wasn’t a friend. I barely knew him. I only guessed at his blood type.”

Sierra gasped.

He shrugged. “I was hoping to save him with my blood long enough so that I could interrogate him. I was worried someone else had gotten to him and the other men I’d hired, and that’s why they were so trigger-happy. Turns out they were just cowards and completely trigger happy. Period. I came here, to this cabin, alone. I’ve been combing the mountains and town trying to hear someone talk about anyone who matched our sister’s description being seen around here. That got me nowhere, so I rented a cabin to lie low until I could think of some other way to find her. I finally got a lucky break. My cabin isn’t far from here. I decided to check out any cabins in the vicinity and when I stood outside listening at one of the windows of this one, I heard Sierra's voice. I headed back to my cabin and called Rafael."

"How did you find out about the tunnel?" Sierra asked.

Beau gave her an impatient look.

She shrugged. "I just wanted to know whether I'm to blame for that. For calling Rafael."

Rafael frowned. "What does calling me have to do with anything?"

"Nothing," Esteban told him. "I found the tunnel because we exhausted every other potential place you two could have been. We found your truck and fanned out from there. It was dumb luck that one of the guys fell on a tree root and into the mouth of the tunnel."

"And you decided it was a good idea to go inside?" Beau asked.

"Last resort. I was desperate and wanted to cross it off my list of potential possibilities of how to find my sister."

Relief swept through Sierra hearing that she hadn't actually compromised their location at the safe house as she'd feared. "Why are you both here?"

"Sierra—" Beau complained.

"I'm done, I'm done. Go ahead with your interrogation."

"Esteban, Rafael, why are you here?"

She jabbed Beau's side.

He winked.

Esteban swore.

"Oh good grief," Rafael said. "I'm here because my sister called, told me my dead brother is actually alive. I'm specifically at this cabin as I already said because Esteban called and told me to meet him here so he could explain everything. Esteban, for the love of God, tell us what the hell is going on and why you pretended to be dead for more than a year and put your family through misery."

Esteban's jaw worked with anger. "Not the entire family. Not Dad."

Sierra sank against Beau's side. "No," she whispered. "Please tell me he's not involved."

"Sorry, sis. Can't."

She bowed her head, tightening her hands into fists.

Beau gently squeezed her hand, then let go. She wanted desperately to cling to him, to take the comfort he'd only briefly offered. But she understood he wanted his right hand free to grab his pistol if he had to, which was sitting beside him at the ready. Still, without even knowing the details, just knowing that her father was mixed up in what was going on made her heart hurt.

"Go on," Rafael urged. "Tell us. We've been living with your lie for months. You owe us the truth, whatever it is. And it had better be the truth if you're going to smear Dad."

Esteban drew a shaky breath before looking Rafael and then Sierra in the eyes. "A few months before I supposedly drowned, I was in Dad's home office. He was at a business meeting and had forgotten some document he needed. So he called me and asked me to scan it on my phone." He shook his head. "It was a contract amendment that could have put millions at risk if he didn't have it signed at that meeting. Some kind of deadline penalty or something. The potential monetary losses are the only reason he allowed me in his desk. Heck, we're not even allowed in his office normally unless he's with us. But he was desperate. He told me where the keys were hidden and told me to get the document from the top drawer."

He fisted his hands. "If he hadn't been so adamant about only opening the top drawer, I never would have opened the others after scanning the document he wanted. But he made me so danged curious about what he might be hiding in that stupid desk. I searched the other drawers. That's when I found out...the truth."

Sierra tensed. "And what's the truth?"

His pain-filled eyes stared at her from across the room. "Mom didn't commit suicide because the cancer treatments weren't going well. The treatments made her sick, sure, but her prognosis—in spite of what Dad later told us—was good. She didn't kill herself. Dad murdered her."

Sierra gasped in shock.

Beau reached for her hand, and this time he didn't let go.

"You're lying," Rafael accused. "He wouldn't do that."

"I'm not lying. Why would I?"

"I don't know. The same reason you've lied to us about being dead for a year."

Esteban and Rafael began shouting at each other.

Sierra sank back against the couch and covered her face.

Beau stood. "Enough." His deep voice cut through the noise. The brothers went silent.

"Fletcher?" Beau asked. "Anything I need to know about?"

"Not unless you want to learn more Spanish insults."

"All right. Esteban, what did you find in the desk? Why do you think your father murdered your mother?"

"I don't think, I know. In the bottom drawer was, well, I guess you'd call it a journal or a diary. It was my mom's. I never knew her to keep anything like that. But the first dated entry was the day she had her biopsy. So I guess she was writing down her thoughts and experiences to help her sort it out or something. I don't know. I felt guilty reading it, but it made me feel kind of...closer to her, you know? Seeing what she went through, how she felt. It wasn't long, maybe fifty pages. I skimmed a lot of it. I was more interested in how she felt at the end, before she...left us. You guys remember that page, front and back, that was found by her body? Her suicide note?"

"It was so sad," Sierra said. "So much talking about her pain and despair."

"Well, lots of pages in her journal were like that. And a lot weren't. The days she was going through side effects from chemo were days she'd write that way. Then she'd start feeling better and talk about her hopes for the future. You get it, right? Dad's the one who supposedly found her suicide note when he found her body. And that supposed note was a torn page from her journal. It wasn't a suicide note at all."

Rafael snorted. "That's your evidence that our father killed our mother? A torn page from her journal? She probably tore it out herself and thought it would be a good way to let us know how she was feeling when she ended things."

"That would make sense," Esteban said, "if she'd been depressed and ready to end it. But she wasn't. The last ten pages, the most recent ones, talked about how well her treatment was going. They spoke about how much better she was feeling and that she would treasure life more going forward. But there was something else in those last ten pages too. She'd fought during her entire marriage to keep us out of the criminal life that Dad leads."

He glanced at Beau, then shrugged. "It's the truth. Everyone knows it." His gaze slid to Sierra. "Even his baby girl who tries to look the other way."

She tightened her hold on Beau's hand. "Because I choose to dwell on the good in him."

He winced. "Rafael and I know him far better than you. We know our real father. Yes, there's good in him. But there's bad too, a whole lot of awful. And in spite of Mom trying to steer us all clear of it, neither Rafael nor I remained as pristine as you. You were Mom's one hope for breaking the cycle. Her sons failed her."

His voice broke, but he quickly sobered. "The other stuff

Mom wrote in those last ten pages, I'm sure, is why Dad killed her. The cancer changed how she looked at things, made her more determined than ever to change us, to save us, basically, to her way of thinking. She wrote that she'd started gathering together documentation ever since her diagnosis that would prove the most egregious crimes our father has committed. She had evidence she was certain could send him to prison for the rest of his life."

"What?" Sierra demanded. "She loved him. She would never—"

"I agree with you," Rafael said. "She wouldn't turn him in."

"I know, I know." Esteban's jaw tightened. "I agree too. But Dad had far too much to lose. I think he was afraid to risk that she might actually do it. Her journal said she was going to tell Dad that if he didn't stop his life of crime and get her sons out of it, she would turn over the evidence to the FBI. That was the last entry in her journal. The day she died."

Rafael and Sierra exchanged pained glances.

"Where is this evidence she had?" Sierra asked.

"I don't know. Her journal said she hid it in a special, safe place. I think what must have happened was that she told Dad what she had and threatened to expose him if he didn't agree to her demands. Dad would have been infuriated, on that we can all agree. He values loyalty above all else. I think he must have flown into a rage and killed her without even thinking about it. Then, to cover it up, he staged her suicide. I imagine he had regrets later, especially when he searched for the evidence she said she'd collected. Mom might have been a poor judge of character, but she was smart about other things. If she said she hid it somewhere safe, she did. I believe it's probably still wherever she put it."

Rafael gave him a hard look. "That's a lot of *if*s, and *I think*s. What can you actually *prove*?"

"I can prove what I said about her getting better, that her prognosis was good. She was beating the cancer and knew it. The journal wasn't the only thing I found in Dad's desk. I found the medical reports from her treatment. I don't have them with me, but I kept them. I can show you later. They prove what I've said."

"About her illness," Sierra said. "But what about Dad… hurting her? Do you have any evidence about that?"

"The empty bottle of pain pills and alleged suicide note were found by Dad with Mom's body. The coroner, knowing Mom was sick with cancer and faced with the note and empty bottle of pills, ruled it a suicide and no autopsy was performed. I didn't want to believe Dad was guilty. I wasn't trying to prove a murder. But I had to know the truth. So I went to the funeral home that took care of her. I spoke to the man who…handled her body, got it ready for the viewing. I asked him if anything seemed out of the ordinary for an overdose death like hers. At first he said no, but I gave him an obscene amount of money, and he told me she had bruises around her throat, big bruises like a man's hand would make. And her eyes were bloodshot. The coroner, not suspecting foul play, probably thought it was a side effect from her treatment. But it wasn't."

"Petechial hemorrhaging," Beau said. "You think he strangled her."

"Yes. The man I spoke to was certain of it. He's handled bodies there for decades and knows the signs."

Sierra shook her head. "But the police, when they came for her body, wouldn't they have seen her eyes, the bruises, and asked questions?"

Beau shook his head. "The bruises probably wouldn't have shown up until the body was sitting awhile. If her eyes were closed, they wouldn't have opened them to check for anything if the suicide staging was convincing enough—mainly because of your father's powerful reputation. Or maybe the police were just plain afraid of him and, since she was allegedly dying of cancer anyway, chose not to dig deeper. They took his word for it."

"Those were my thoughts too," Esteban said. "It's why I bribed the funeral guy to tell me the truth as he saw it. She was definitely murdered. And the only person who could have done it was Dad. Proving she was murdered is actually the easy part. She was embalmed and buried. An exhumation would show the bruises under her makeup, the blood in her eyes, maybe damage to the bones in her throat. They might even be able to test her body somehow to see whether any of the pain medication was actually in her system. But even without that, I think the bruises and eyes would be enough to prove strangulation as the cause of death."

"I agree," Beau said. "But then you have to prove he's the one who did it. That's a different legal battle altogether, even if we all agree it sounds like he's the perpetrator."

Sierra sat in stunned silence. Rafael was quiet too. Esteban hung his head, obviously miserable that he'd had to tell them such painful news.

"Just a few more questions," Beau said, his voice somber. "First, how did your father discover that you knew the truth?"

"I think…he must have set a trap, something in his desk drawers, to show him if anyone ever opened them. He somehow knew I'd gone not just in the top drawer, but the others too. Or maybe he realized I'd taken the journal and medical reports. That was stupid of me. I made copies and was going to put them back a few days later, when he left on another business trip. But when I went to put them back, the locks had been changed on his drawers. The very next day is when the attacks began."

"Attacks?" Beau asked.

"Someone ran me off the road. I was lucky. Came away with only a few scratches. There were other close calls, things that would look like accidents if I was killed. I could see it in his eyes too, when I'd come over for dinners with the family. He knew. And he hated me for it. I think that since Sierra and Rafael didn't act differently or do anything to raise his suspicions, he realized I hadn't told them yet. I wanted all my ducks in a row, all the evidence, including what Mom hid about Dad, before going to them to share what I knew. But then I started worrying that if I told them, he'd kill them too. As much as he knows how, he loves us. But he loves his money and freedom more. If those were put at risk, he'd stop at nothing to protect himself. Don't you agree, Rafael?"

"I agree. We're all a family, close, tight. But the three of us are still different from the others. You and I have done things we're not proud of. But not like our other brothers who are deeply entrenched in Dad's seamy side of the business. And of course, Sierra has never been a part of any of that. If any of us could ever be seen as a threat, it would be us three. He knows how much we adored Mom, that we'd want to bring him to justice if we believed he'd killed her. That alone would make us a threat if we found out. So yes, I believe he'd sacrifice us to keep himself safe."

Sierra cleared her throat. "As much as I hate to admit it, I agree. What happened after that, Esteban? You faked a drowning and put another man's body in the lake to keep Dad's men from continuing to search for you? If so, why go after Beau? Why go after me?"

His eyes widened. "I didn't go after you, sis. I swear. But, yes, I faked my death. The supposed friends with me on the boat were low-level criminals I hired to play a part. They didn't even know my real identity. I thought by faking my death that I'd finally be safe, that Dad would stop sending men to search for me. And it worked. No close calls after that. None of Dad's men nosing around. Months later my money was running out because I couldn't access my accounts without tipping Dad off that I was still alive. So I began my own businesses. And I needed guys to help me…uh, run it."

"You started your own life of crime like your father's," Beau accused.

He shrugged. "I was used to living the good life, having money. I didn't know how to live any other way. I was lazy, made money the old-fashioned way. Crime."

"Then, why return to Mystic Lake?" Beau asked. "Why attack my cabin?"

"Part of making sure I was still safe from my dad was to come here every few months to see if anything was going on around the lake or town that might indicate they were still searching for me. I wanted to make sure that Dad believed I was dead. The last time I came here, I heard people talking in that big restaurant downtown—"

"Stella's," Beau said.

"Right, Stella's. They mentioned some pretty Spanish lady who was going around town asking about a boat crash earlier. I suspected that might be Sierra. I was terrified that if Dad's men ever came here, like I do, to make sure things are still quiet and under control, that they'd hear about that woman and would tell Dad. I also heard that the police chief was digging into cold cases, which likely would include mine since officially my body was never found."

He shook his head. "It was a nightmare. I had to worry about Dad, the police chief, and Sierra too. If Dad thought for one minute that I was actually alive, and that Sierra was looking for me, he'd be worried we'd get together and I'd tell her about Mom. He'd already tried to kill me. I knew he wouldn't hesitate to kill her if he considered her a threat. Everything I did after that was to protect her."

"And you," Beau accused.

"And me. Yes. I wanted to shut down her investigation, and yours. But I wasn't sure how. I wanted her safe, not hurt. I swear. So I watched, waited, tried to find out what either of you knew. That's why I sent those men to your cabin, Dawson. They were supposed to gather information. But I made a huge mistake. I never told them about Sierra. So when she and that second cop showed up, that ruined the plan. They shot at her too, not realizing they shouldn't have put her in danger."

Sierra jerked her head up. "They shot at me *too*? What does *too* mean? They weren't there to steal a laptop, were they? They were there to kill Beau but Officer Collier and I showed up with him, ruining your planned murder. That's what you meant. Isn't it, Esteban?"

Rafael groaned. "Brother, please tell us you didn't do something that stupid. Tell us you weren't planning to kill police."

Esteban's jaw tightened. He didn't answer.

"I almost hate you right now," Sierra told him.

He nodded, as if it was what he'd expect. "I messed up. A lot. But I swear I was trying to protect you, and Rafael. I was prepared to live on my own and never see either of you again so that Dad would never think I told you about Mom."

"What about the man who really died the day you faked your death?" she asked. "Did you kill him?"

His eyes flew open wide. "What? No. No, I didn't. I staged my drowning, paid off my fake witnesses to corroborate the story. But when Dad's guys kept showing up searching for me, and then he hired a company to search the lake, I knew I had to do something to convince them I really was dead. So I bribed a guy to dig up a skeleton in what the police call paupers' graves, where no one claims a body and the city puts it in a pine box without a funeral or anything and buries them. He was a John Doe. I put my clothes and stuff on him and sank the body. I wasn't sure what would happen, but it worked. I saw the company that was searching for my remains take the body. I made my way to Memphis later and saw the headstone with my name on it in our family cemetery. I thought I was in the clear until I heard about Sierra trying to prove I was murdered." He shook his head. "Why did you have to go do that, Sierra? That ruined everything."

Beau pointed his finger at him. "Listen here, Covington. Don't blame your sister for your screw-ups. If you'd gone to the police about your father murdering your mother, Sierra would have never come here trying to get justice for the brother she loved and refused to accept had simply drowned. She was trying to honor your memory. Nothing that has happened is her fault. That's on you."

Esteban fell silent, then whispered, "Sorry, Sierra."

She ignored him and looked up at Beau. "Thank you."

He squeezed her hand, then sighed heavily.

"What now?" she asked.

"I'm just thinking about where we go from here. If your father was anyone other than Michael Covington, this would be a simple matter of involving the police and providing them any evidence we can to prove everything Esteban has stated. Then your father would go to jail like anyone else. But it's more complicated than that."

Sierra's brothers both nodded their agreement.

Sierra frowned. "Why? I don't follow."

Beau holstered his pistol, apparently deciding her brothers were no longer a threat. He turned on the couch to face her.

"The FBI has been trying to bring down your family for decades. A journal, a medical report, the testimony of your brother about the attacks, even the testimony of the man from the funeral home is nothing compared to the evidence they've had against him for numerous other crimes. And yet, they've never even gotten to the point of being able to arrest him for any crimes. If we can't get a conviction, we can't ensure the safety of your brothers, or you. You'll be on the run for the rest of your lives."

He gently feathered her hair back from her face. "Even if I'm your bodyguard, I can't guarantee your safety against a man with your father's resources."

She swallowed and clung to his hand. "Then, what do we do?"

Rafael shook his head. "I don't know that we really can do anything. We're doomed to go on the run, like Chief Dawson says."

Beau looked at the phone sitting on the coffee table. He slowly got up and retrieved it. "Fletcher, you still there?"

"I am. And I wish I had a suggestion for you. But I don't. I think this might come down to a WITSEC situation, don't you?"

"WITSEC," Sierra asked. "What does she mean by that?"

"Officially," Beau said, "it's the Witness Security Program. But most people know it by the more colloquial term *witness protection.* In return for testifying for the FBI in a case like this, the Feds would give you a new identity and settle you into a new life somewhere else to keep you safe."

"But…that means giving up your entire life as you know it, right? Never seeing people you know again?" she asked.

"It does. But before you worry about that, consider that you have nothing to bargain with. Your brothers, maybe. You, nothing. You haven't been involved in your father's illegal side. So you don't have anything to offer to the FBI. But I don't see a point in even going down that rabbit hole because, as I said before, your dad gets out of everything the FBI throws at him. WITSEC isn't the answer here."

"Then, what is?" she asked. "There has to be something we can do."

He shook his head. "I'm sorry, Sierra." Then he winked.

She stared at him in confusion.

"Fletcher, I'm ending the call now. Thanks for your help. At this point, while we think this through, let's cancel tonight's status meeting. And there's no reason for you all to come out here. I'm not pressing charges against Esteban. Sierra, do you want to press charges?"

She frowned. "Um, no?"

"I'm hanging up now, Fletcher."

"Sorry about how things turned out," she said. "We'll brainstorm here and talk to you tomorrow."

Beau ended the call and pulled out his pocketknife. He cut the cord tying Rafael's hands, then took off Esteban's handcuffs.

They both gave him grateful looks and rubbed their wrists.

When he sat again, Sierra looked up at him. "You really think this is hopeless?"

"There might be another option. But I didn't want to say it in front of Fletcher." He grimaced. "I can't believe I'm even considering this. It goes against everything I've always stood for as far as following the law to the letter."

"Beau, whatever it is, don't." Sierra shook her head. "If helping us means you have to cross that line, please don't. You'd end up hating me down the road, blaming me for compromising your principles. And I couldn't live with myself for doing that to you."

"He has an idea," Esteban said. "Let the man talk."

"Shut up, Esteban," she and Rafael both said.

He rolled his eyes and sank against the back of the couch.

"I'm not finished." Beau turned to face Sierra. "If the law can't protect you, then what's the point of having laws? I got into this business to protect people, to get justice. And in this case, the law and justice are two completely different things. True justice would mean prosecuting your father for your mother's death. I'm not sure I can do anything to get that justice for you, and I'm really sorry about that. But there might be something we can do to get justice for you and your brothers. Meaning, there might be a way to secure your protection so you can go on living your lives and not be afraid."

She frowned. "How?"

"We do what your mother tried to do."

"I don't—wait, are you talking about the evidence she hid?"

"That's exactly what I'm talking about. We need to find that evidence. If we read her journal, maybe we can find clues that help us understand where she hid the evidence. Even if the journal doesn't help, we can search anywhere you and your brothers believe she might have hidden the documentation. It would be somewhere not too far away so she could access it. But it would be somewhere your father wouldn't think to look. Esteban, you said she mentioned in the journal that she put it somewhere, what, *special*? Is that the exact word she used?"

"*A special, safe place.* That's what she wrote."

"Did your mother ever spend much time outside your property? Maybe with friends in another town?"

"Not really. I mean, the country club, some. Church, of course. Mainly, though, she was content to stay home and paint or do gardening."

"A garden. That would be special to her. Would your father think to search there?"

"Probably. It seems a little too obvious." This time it was Rafael who spoke. "She also loved the library, the one in the mansion. It's huge, three stories tall. There are probably over a million books in there." His eyes widened. "Dad isn't much of a reader. And even if he thought the evidence was there, I can't see him spending the time to search that many books. He wouldn't trust anyone else to search either. He wouldn't want to risk them finding the evidence and using it against him."

"Your father might think that it's in there," Beau replied. "But given what you said, he may feel it's safer there than anywhere else. As long as he has the mansion, the evidence won't go anywhere. That's where I'd look."

"Then, what?" Sierra asked. "We go to the FBI?"

"That's one option. It's the option I would have chosen, before we had this conversation. But the wheels of justice move slowly. I worry it will take too long to go that route. The FBI will take years following up on whatever your mother has, authenticating it, corroborating it, before making a move. We need to secure yours and your brothers' safety now. We don't *go* to the FBI. We *threaten* to go to the FBI, use the documentation as our bargaining chip. And we do it together, as a team having each other's backs, so that what happened to your mother doesn't happen to us."

He feathered his hand down the side of her face, ignoring Esteban's curses. "Tomorrow morning, bright and early, we're all going to Memphis. We'll use that bolt-hole you mentioned at the mansion to gain entrance and search the library. And if we're right, if we find your mother's documents there, we'll have our leverage. Then we'll make a deal with the devil."

"Chief Dawson?"

He glanced at Rafael in question.

"What if we can't find the evidence?"

"Plan B, of course."

"What's plan B?" Sierra asked.

He grimaced. "I wish I knew."

"I'm sure you'll think of something. You always do."

He didn't appear to be convinced.

She wasn't either. The task before them seemed nearly impossible. "Beau, I haven't seen either of my brothers in a while, especially Esteban, of course. Do you mind giving us some privacy so we can catch up?"

"Of course. Esteban, Rafael, you're welcome to stay here overnight. Both of the couches are big and comfortable. There are extra linens in the hall closet. Or you can meet us here at dawn if you prefer. Sierra and I don't have a car at this cabin. Do either of you have one close by?"

"I do," Rafael said. "My rental I drove from the airport. We can use that."

"And I've got a cabin near here already," Esteban said, looking uncomfortable as he glanced from Sierra to Beau. "If you two are, uh, staying here, I'd prefer to stay there. Rafael can stay with me."

"Fair enough. I'll watch TV in the bedroom, give you three your time alone."

As soon as the bedroom door closed, Sierra pulled the coffee table close to the couch where her brothers were and sat on the table facing them. And this time, she spoke only in Spanish, just in case Beau heard them.

"Beau isn't going to the mansion with us tomorrow," she whispered.

Esteban did a fist pump. "Good. You've seen the light. You're going to dump the cop."

She poked him in the ribs. "I'm not dumping him. But he'll probably dump me after this. I think he's right about what we need to do, find the evidence, make a deal with Dad. I honestly don't see another viable option. But this is a mess of our making, not his. I've been in denial my entire adult life, trying to pretend Dad isn't as bad as we all know he is. And you two have gone right along with him, ignoring all the advice from Mom."

When they both started to argue, she held up a hand to stop them. "I don't want Beau coming along because I don't want him getting hurt, or worse, if this plan doesn't go the way we hope it will."

"What do you need us to do?" Esteban rubbed his hands together as if in anticipation. "Tie him to a concrete block and toss him in the lake?"

She gasped in horror.

"Kidding. Damn, don't take me so seriously."

Rafael elbowed him.

"Ouch. Stop it, you two. I'm going to have bruises."

"Neither of you does anything to hurt Beau. Swear it," she said.

"I swear." Rafael looked at his brother. "Your turn."

"Fine. As much as I'd like to, I won't hurt the cop."

"Any cop. That's rule number one."

"Yeah, yeah, whatever."

She rolled her eyes. "You two are hopeless. But we're in this together. I'll meet you out front at three."

"Why so early?" Esteban complained.

"Because it's a long drive to Memphis, and I want to be there and get the deal made before Beau could catch up to us."

"How?" Rafael asked. "How will you sneak out without him knowing? Cops have a sixth sense about these things. He'll probably wake up the second you open the door."

Her heart heavy, she said, "Leave that to me."

Chapter Nineteen

Beau came awake with a start, surprised to see daylight seeping in through the window blinds. It definitely wasn't dawn. He'd overslept by at least an hour, judging by the light. He sat up, then groaned and lay back down. The room seemed to be spinning around him. He was light-headed, dizzy. He closed his eyes and drew slow deep breaths. What the heck was wrong with him?

"Sierra?" He reached out toward her, but his fingers only touched air. "Sierra?"

He opened his eyes, wincing at the still-spinning room. The bed was empty. The bathroom—she must be in the bathroom, probably mad as a hornet that he'd overslept. He smiled at the anticipation of seeing her eyes narrow and her hair bouncing around her shoulders as she yelled at him in a mixture of English and Spanish.

Wait. Her brothers were supposed to meet them here at dawn. Was everyone in the living room, letting him sleep? They were wasting time. Including the hour it would take just to reach Chattanooga from Mystic Lake, it would take nearly seven hours to drive to their father's home on the outskirts of Memphis. He'd mapped out the route last night. They should have been on the road long before now.

He threw back the covers and swung his legs over the side, groaning when a bout of nausea had him breathing fast and hard. When he finally felt like he could move without throwing up, he opened his eyes. The room wasn't spinning anymore. But he still felt like hell. What was going on?

It wasn't like he'd stayed up late partying and drinking. Well, he'd had one drink. Sierra had brought it in when she came to bed and… His gaze flew to the nightstand. There was his drink, or what was left of it. And sitting beside it was a note.

His stomach sank with dread even before he read it. He already knew what it would say.

Beau, I hope you can find it in your heart to forgive me. Or at least understand. I care about you too much to let you risk your life in this mess my brother created. No, not my brother, my father. This is his fault. He's an evil man to have taken away the precious gift that my mother was. I couldn't bear it if he took you away too. I'm so, so sorry I ever dragged you into this. But now I'm getting you out.

I put a little allergy medicine in your drink last night to make you sleep. Drink water and take a hot shower to help you feel better in the morning. I didn't see any other way to keep you safe. Please don't follow us to Memphis. We're leaving at three, so obviously we'll have a huge head start. By the time you get there, it will all be over. I'm almost positive I know exactly where my mom would have hidden the evidence in the library. I know her favorite books, and there's an inspirational poetry volume she loved called Safe and Secure. *Pretty obvious, right? I think she did that on purpose, put that hint about safety and security in her journal in case things didn't go as planned. Everything's going to be okay.*

When I see you again, the bargain will be made, and we'll all be safe.
Forgive me. Sierra.

Beau swore viciously and hurried to the bathroom, bumping into furniture as he went. He dropped to his knees in front of the toilet and shoved his finger down his throat, forcing himself to throw up. A splash of water on his hair and face helped wake him up. After quickly taking care of his other needs and brushing his teeth, he threw his clothes on. A shower would have been great, as Sierra had recommended, but he didn't have time to spare.

After grabbing a burner phone and his pistol and shoving an extra magazine in his pocket, he jogged into the living room. As soon as he reached it, he stopped. They'd left at three. He didn't even have a car, just the boat tied up at the dock. And Mystic Lake was landlocked. The boat was useless.

Think, dang it. Think. How could he get to Memphis in time to keep those three fools from getting themselves killed? He thought about calling the Memphis police, but quickly discarded that idea. Getting police involved would mean there'd be no way to make that bargain with Michael Covington. Without that bargain, they were as good as dead. How could he get there in time to stop them?

A commercial flight could work, in theory. He quickly calculated in his mind the drive time to the airport, the duration of the flight. The math worked, but only if there was no traffic, no delays at the airport, a flight leaving just when he needed it, no lines at a car rental agency and no traffic around Memphis. And he wouldn't be able to bring his gun. He shook his head. No way. Too many variables. Heck, he didn't even have a car to get out of Mystic Lake to begin with. Nix the commercial flight idea. What else? How could he get there on time, or better yet, early enough to get the documentation and make the deal before Sierra and the others even arrived?

He blinked. Of course. That was it. He clawed for his cell phone and quickly punched in a familiar set of numbers.

The line clicked. "Mystic Lake Marina, Bobby speaking."

"Bobby, it's former Police Chief Beau Dawson. I need a favor."

SIERRA CLUTCHED THE thick packet of papers to her chest and stepped out of her father's office, closing the door behind her. She looked to her left at Rafael, then to her right at Esteban.

"We did it," she whispered.

"We did," Rafael agreed.

Esteban remained silent.

"Let's get out of here before he calls his men to come to the mansion and they try to take the papers from us," Rafael whispered. "We need to get it hidden before that can happen. That's the only way the bargain we just made will keep us safe." He led the way to the back hall where they would exit through the bolt-hole the same way they'd arrived.

Rafael pressed the panel in the wall, and it clicked open, revealing the dark tunnel beyond. Sierra followed him inside, with Esteban behind her. Lights would come on once they were about twenty feet in, by design. That way if it was dark in the house, no one would see the light shining around the panel.

The lights flipped on.

She jumped in surprise to see a man standing in front of them, blocking their way.

"Beau, I don't—what are you doing here? How did you get here so fast?"

"Plan B," he growled. "Helicopter. I commandeered the town's medevac chopper hoping to get here in time to save your pretty neck. What the hell were you thinking?" He glared at Rafael. "What were *you* thinking, letting your sister put herself in danger this way?" He paused, then looked down at the stack of papers in Sierra's hands. "You found it?"

"We did," she said. "Right where I thought it would be. How do you feel? Are you okay? Dizzy?"

"I was. Thanks to you. Just how many allergy pills did you put in that drink to make me that sick?"

She winced. "I'm sorry. I really am. But I'd do it all over again to keep you safe. My brothers and I made the deal with my father. He agreed to leave us alone, to not send anyone after us as long as we never turn over the evidence to the FBI or any other agency. He was hurt and angry, but he agreed."

Beau let out a deep breath, then pulled her close. "Don't ever scare me like that again. Things could have gone completely wrong. It was a sketchy plan at best. I wanted to be the one to do the negotiating, to keep you out of danger."

She hugged him tight. "I know. But it worked out. It's over."

He kissed her, a quick fierce kiss before stepping back. "This isn't the way I wanted it, but what's done is done. Let's go." He took her hand and they started down the hidden passageway.

"Wait," Rafael called out from behind them. "Where's Esteban?"

They stopped and turned around. "He was just here," Sierra said. "Esteban," she whispered toward the darkened section of the tunnel. "Esteban, come on."

Rafael jogged into the dark. A moment later he called out. "He's not in the passageway."

Sierra took off running.

"Sierra, stop!" Beau yelled behind her.

She shoved Rafael out of her way and threw the secret panel open, slipping and sliding on the marble floor as she rounded the corner toward her father's office.

"Stop!" Rafael and Beau both yelled, their footsteps pounding in the hallway.

She ran faster, adrenaline and panic giving her a burst of speed.

Bam! Bam!

Her heart sank at the sound of gunshots coming from behind the double doors in her father's office. She yanked out the gun she'd taken from Beau again and threw open the doors, then stopped in shock just inside.

"No!" she screamed, staring in horror at her father standing by his desk with a gun in his hand. And there, on the floor in front of the desk, Esteban lay in a bloody heap, eyes closed.

"You bastard," Rafael yelled, running past her, firing his gun.

Her father jerked back, blood beginning to seep from his shoulder even as he fired at Rafael.

Rafael silently fell to the floor, dropping beside Esteban, bleeding.

Sierra screamed again.

Beau's footsteps sounded right behind her.

She dodged away from him, escaping his outstretched hand as he tried to stop her, and turned her gun on her father.

As if in slow motion, she saw her father swinging around, sweeping his pistol toward her.

She tightened her finger on the trigger.

Something slammed against her. She squeezed the trigger as she fell to the ground, but her shot went wide.

Bam! Bam! Bam!

She shoved herself up from the floor, bringing up her gun again, then froze.

There was no one to shoot. Her father's body was draped across the desk, blood dripping from his hair. His gun lay on the rug beside his desk where it must have fallen when he was shot. Beau. He must have shoved her out of the way and shot her father.

She whirled around. He wasn't there. "Beau? Beau?"

A low groan had her looking down. There, just past one of the wing chairs, he was on his side, his face contorted in pain.

"Oh my God. No, Beau." She threw her pistol down and ran to him, dropping to her knees and turning his face toward her with shaking hands.

Jeremy, her father's housekeeper, ran into the office. "What's happening? What's going on?"

"Call 911," she told him. "We need an ambulance and police. Hurry."

His eyes widened as he looked past her.

"Jeremy, call 911. Now!"

He whirled around and ran out of the office.

"Beau?" She ran her hands up and down his chest, searching for injuries. There, a small hole in his shirt. A bullet hole. Her entire body began to shake.

He blinked and looked up at her. Before she could say anything else, he shoved her down on the floor and brought his pistol up, aiming toward the desk.

"Your aim was true," she whispered. "He's gone. It's over."

He lowered his pistol and struggled to sit up.

"Don't," she pleaded. "You've been shot. Jeremy's calling for an ambulance."

"I don't need one." He tore open his shirt. "I put a Kevlar vest on beneath my shirt so your father wouldn't know I was wearing one when I confronted him. Hurts like a son of a gun, but I'm okay." His expression turned from pain to fury. "Remind me to yell at you later for almost getting yourself killed. Right now I need to check on your brothers."

He shoved himself to his feet, then stopped her when she tried to go with him.

"Don't. Let me do it. Please, Sierra. Wait right here and let me check them first. Okay?"

She swallowed, closing her eyes when Beau bent down to check Rafael for a pulse.

"Please, please, please," she whispered, not even sure what she was asking for. She'd seen the blood, the carnage. She knew what to expect. But part of her refused to believe it. She clung to a tiny glimmer of hope that at least one of her brothers was still alive.

Until Beau returned, his face pale, and pulled her into his arms.

Her knees buckled. He scooped her up and strode out of the office with her in his arms, quietly sobbing against his chest.

Chapter Twenty

Sierra rubbed her arms up and down her coat sleeves as she looked down at the hard ground. November had roared into Mystic Lake like a freight train, bringing frigid temperatures not usually seen until mid-January. The cold winds had swept across the Smokies, sweeping away much of the fading fall foliage and the leaf-peeper tourists who'd been swarming across the area. Unfortunately, the colder temperatures hadn't managed to chase away the more obnoxious types in town—reporters. But even they were beginning to give up their quest to pressure Sierra into answering their unending questions about her family and everything that had happened. Not because of the weather, because of Beau. He was tenacious in his protectiveness of her.

He'd been nothing short of wonderful, keeping the media away as much as possible whenever the two of them were in town. And moving Sierra up the mountain to his secluded cabin to give her even more privacy, with the perk of being with him as well, which she would have thoroughly enjoyed at any other time.

Simply getting up every day had seemed like an impossible task at first. But Beau refused to let her sulk and give up on life. He wouldn't let her sleep all day and wallow. He got her up, carried her into the shower if she wouldn't walk on her own. Dressed her. Fed her. Held her for hours on end as she cried against him. She'd cursed him in English and Spanish. He'd simply kissed her and held her some more.

Little by little, she'd come alive again. Now, months later, she was coping. Happy even, as far as being with Beau. It was wonderful having him around every day. And the stress of being her father's daughter, stress she hadn't even realized she'd had, was lifted now. She was just an ordinary person who no longer had to make excuses for her family.

But that didn't mean she didn't miss them. She was learning to move on, but she'd never get over the loss. Instead, she had to figure out a new normal. Because life without her family would never be the same as it once had been. That was both good and bad. These days, because of Beau, more good than bad.

She enjoyed living in his cabin. It was homey, welcoming, much more cozy than the Covington mansion had ever been. And it was beautiful again. All signs of the gunfight that had taken place there had been eliminated, except for the scars on the log walls that would only fade with time. Beau had replaced not only the broken windows but *all* of the cabin's windows and even the sliders on the back deck with strong, bulletproof glass. While he didn't expect any trouble, he was determined to do everything he could to always keep her safe.

Sierra shook her head in wonder. Even her cranky moods and bouts of crying when the loss of her family became too overwhelming didn't scare him away. He seemed to care about her deeply, although he'd never said it. Then again, her father had told her hundreds of times that he loved her, and in the end, he'd loved himself and his money more than his family.

She dabbed at her wet eyes before more tears could fall. She detested tears. They made her feel weak, vulnerable. Being vulnerable was the worst feeling of all. But it was so hard knowing she'd never see her biological brothers again. She'd never see her other brothers again either, except for visiting them in prison. Assuming she could ever convince them to actually allow her to visit.

So far they hadn't.

All four of them—Thomas, Vincent, Anthony and Charles—had made plea deals to avoid longer prison sentences. But they'd still be old men by the time they got out. They blamed her for that, especially since she'd managed to avoid any charges at all. They also blamed her for their father's death, of course. She couldn't fault them for that. She had her own guilt to deal with over his loss. But knowing he'd murdered her mother and two of her brothers went a long way toward assuaging that guilt. The final nail in the proverbial coffin of her relationship with her remaining brothers was that they resented that the FBI had seized all of their assets while Sierra had retained hers.

She had her mother to thank for that.

Her mother's insistence that only legally obtained money and properties flowed to her children meant that the FBI had no legal claims to Sierra's holdings. Sierra's financial independence was her mother's legacy, and it would have been for her biological brothers as well if they'd stayed fully on the legal side of her father's businesses. The FBI was able to argue that there was no way to distinguish legal from illegal gains when it came to Rafael and Esteban, so the government had taken it all instead of allowing any of it to pass to Sierra. Not that it mattered. She didn't need their money. And she'd give up everything she had if it would mean that she could spend even one more day with them or her mother.

"I love you, Mom. Rafael. Esteban. I miss you so dang much."

Her hands shook as she placed a single red rose on top of each of the three graves. In spite of the FBI seizing her father's estates, including his mansion in Memphis, they'd deeded the family cemetery to her in exchange for the documentation her mother had collected.

She'd had a new, fancy headstone made for Jack Wilson's grave, the man who'd originally been buried with Esteban's name. Mr. Wilson was now given the dignity in death that he'd been denied in life.

She'd had her father buried in the Memphis family cemetery too, alongside his parents and a long line of Covington ancestors. But the idea of burying her brothers there, or leaving her mother with the man who'd killed her, was impossible to accept. While she'd mulled over her options, Beau had done the unexpected.

He'd offered to have all three of them buried on his mountain property here in Mystic Lake.

It was remote, protected from curious onlookers. And it allowed her to visit them any time she wanted. It was an offer she couldn't refuse.

Straightening, she whispered a quick prayer for her siblings and mother, and even one for her father. After everything he'd done, after stealing her family from her, she still couldn't pretend he'd never existed. So many of her treasured memories included him. He'd done so much good for her and her family through the years. She remembered and cherished that side of him, in spite of hating the way he'd ended things. It was an emotional tug of war inside her. All she could hope was that time would continue to erode the pain and help her find peace. Time and Beau.

Smiling at the thought of her fierce protector, she headed down the winding path that he'd cut through the woods that ended at the front of his cabin.

He was waiting there for her.

He got up from one of the rocking chairs he'd bought because she'd mentioned she thought it would be nice to sit on the porch and look at the fall foliage when the cool breezes made sitting on the exposed back deck too chilly. His shiny boots reflected the morning light as he jogged down the steps to greet her with a smile just as bright. His leather police-issued jacket hung open revealing his crisply ironed button-up shirt and the dress pants that could have stood on their own from the sharp creases.

"Looking extremely handsome this morning, Chief Dawson." She plucked an imaginary piece of lint off his collar and smoothed it down. "Ready for your first day back at the job? I know Chris will be ecstatic to finally pass the reins over to you."

He pressed a whisper-soft kiss against her lips. "Collier and everyone else. They call me complaining nearly every day, as you well know. Collier's sick of the paperwork and meetings with town leadership, especially the novice new mayor who was voted into office after that recall vote on our previous mayor. Or so Collier says."

"You don't believe him?"

He shrugged. "Collier did great as the chief. He was also partly responsible for convincing the Jerichos to settle their lawsuit against the town, allowing me to be rehired as chief and using their settlement to fund us looking into our cold cases, especially those involving missing persons. If it wasn't for Collier, we'd probably still be fighting that lawsuit. And I certainly wouldn't be the chief again. Everyone knows Collier made all that happen, in spite of their teasing. But he's restless, always has been. It seems worse now. Maybe the responsibility was too constricting for an adventurer sort like him. Who knows." His dark eyes searched hers. "Are you sure you want me to go back to work? I can put them off a little longer."

"No. It's time. We both have to move on. And I'm excited for you to get back in law enforcement. I'm so happy your town leaders and team didn't let the Covington name and what happened keep them from asking you to return."

He frowned. "*What happened* is that you've always lived a law-abiding, exemplary life and brought honor to your family name. You did everything right, and you're the reason I was given another chance at being chief. Anyone who doesn't understand that or judges you for what others did isn't worth our time."

She smoothed the front of his shirt.

His frown deepened. "You've been crying again."

She wiped her cheeks. "Only a little. I'm getting better every day, trying to focus on the happy times instead of how everything ended. I don't think I could have survived these past few months without being able to lean on you. But you have to be getting tired of having me taking up space in your cabin. Even though I'm a friend with benefits." She waggled her brows.

He laughed, then, as if he couldn't help himself, he kissed her again. "The benefits definitely outweigh the tirades of broken English you subject me to."

She rolled her eyes. "Broken English, ha. My English is perfect. It's your Spanish that needs improvement."

"Truth. I'm working on it, *mi amor*." He slid his fingers through her hair. "I'll never get tired of having you here with me. And I'm here for you to lean on as long as you want. Always."

She tilted her head. "Always? Careful. I might take you up on that."

He arched a brow. "Really?"

"*Pfft.* Have I been subtle and didn't realize it?"

He laughed, then grew serious, his gaze searching hers as if he was debating something.

She frowned. "What?"

"Hold that thought." He jogged up the steps and rushed into the cabin.

Sierra fisted her hands by her sides. Every time she started to broach the subject of the future and what it might hold for them, he managed to change the subject. Was it on purpose or not? She wasn't sure. She trudged up the porch steps to one of the rocking chairs. But before she could sit, the front door opened and Beau hurried outside, stopping in front of her.

"Is something wrong?" she asked.

He shook his head. "No. Everything's finally right. I don't know what I was waiting for except, well, I wanted to make this perfect. But this is the first time since…everything, that we'll be apart for more than a few hours. And although that will be hard, it also makes me deliriously happy knowing you'll be here when I come home. That got me thinking, maybe now is that perfect time I've been waiting for."

She stared at him, afraid to hope. "Deliriously happy? You've never spoken like that before. Perfect time? For what?" She teasingly pressed the back of her hand to his forehead. "Are you running a fever?"

He pulled her hand down and kissed it. "No. And I'm sorry I've never told you that before, how happy you make me. Because you do make me happy. And I hope I make you happy. And, well—"

"Beau?"

"Hmm?"

She swallowed against the tightness in her throat. "If this is leading up to something big and amazing, and I really hope it is, would you please get on with it? *Madre de Dios*, you're so slow."

He grinned and pulled a small black velvet box out of the pocket of his jacket before getting down on one knee.

Her entire body flushed with heat. It took all of her self-control not to jump up and down. “Finally. *¡Apúrate!*”

He was laughing as he opened the box and held it up for her to see the gorgeous teardrop solitaire diamond ring with a smaller circle of diamonds surrounding it.

“Yes!” She hopped from foot to foot, unable to contain her excitement any longer as she held out her hand with her ring finger at the ready.

He grinned. “You can't say *yes*. I haven't asked you anything yet.”

“Then, ask!”

“Stop jumping, little rabbit.”

“I can't help it. Just ask me already.”

“Sierra Theresa Covington, would you please do me the extreme honor of becoming my wife?”

“I thought we'd never get to this part. *Sí, Sí*, yes. I'll marry you. Duh.”

His eyes danced with laughter as he slid the ring onto her finger.

She tugged her hand from his and turned it toward the sun, angling it back and forth, watching the diamonds sparkle. “I was beginning to think I'd have to be the one asking. You took your sweet time. I was going to—*ooomph.*”

His mouth covered hers, and he swept her into the sweetest, hottest kiss she'd ever had. When he finally pulled back, she stared up at him in wonder, slightly out of breath. “Okaaay. Does this…does this mean you love me?”

His eyes widened in dismay, his expression turning serious. Ever so gently, he cupped her face with his hands. “Have I never told you?”

“I guarantee I would have remembered if you had.”

He briefly squeezed his eyes shut as if in pain. “I'm so, so sorry about that. I think about how much I love you all the time. I honestly hadn't realized I'd never said it out loud." He stared down at her in wonder. "I love you, Sierra. And I've never loved anyone, not like this." He kissed her left cheek. "I love you." He kissed her right cheek. "I love you." He kissed the top of her head and pulled her against him, hugging her, his love for her seeping into her skin and warming her heart. "I love you."

"I love you too," she whispered.

He made a choking sound in his throat and tightened his arms around her.

She endured the smothering embrace as long as she could, then slapped her hands against his sides and strained against him.

He let go and stepped back. "What's wrong?"

"I couldn't breathe."

"Sorry. I got caught up in the moment. You've never told me you loved me before either."

"Yes, well. According to my mama, the man has to say it first. Now that you have, I'll say it more often."

"Good to know." He reached for her.

She quickly scooted back. "No, no. Now that we're going to get married, there are rules you have to agree to follow."

His expression turned wary. "Rules?"

"What's good for the swan and all that."

His mouth crooked in a half smile. "Goose. Not swan. *What's good for the goose is good for the gander.*"

She waved her hand in the air. "Whatever. What rule number are we up to?"

He crossed his arms. "There are only three rules, and you darn well know it."

"Three. Right. Rule number four, then. No more thinking these *I love you*s in your mind and not sharing them. You have to say it, tell me that you love me. At least twice every day."

"Twice?"

"Once in the morning when we wake up. And once at night before we go to bed. Even if you're mad at me. You have to always tell me you love me. And you have to mean it."

"I can handle that. I love you, Sierra. And I mean it. I always will."

"That one doesn't count as one of your two today."

He grinned. "Of course not. What's the next rule?"

"Oh. That was it. Just rule number four. It's the most important rule of all."

"No. There's another one that's even more important. Rule number five."

She put her hands on her hips. "Five? You don't get to make up another rule. You already have three of them!"

He tilted her chin up and softly ran his thumb across her lower lip. "Rule number five. Never, ever put yourself in danger on purpose like you did the day you snuck off to confront your father. We're in this together, from this day forward. For better, for worse, we have to be honest and trust each other. No matter what."

"Dang it." She wiped her face. "My eyes are leaking again. I agree to all your rules. Now, hurry up and go to work so you can come back home. We have things to do tonight, new things, to celebrate."

He blinked. His Adam's apple bobbed up and down in his throat. "New things?"

"Oh yes. Things you'll like. Very, very much." She winked.

His voice was hoarse when he spoke again. "Rule number six."

"No! No more rules."

He pulled his phone out and slapped it into her palm before scooping her up in his arms.

"Rule number six," he repeated. "When your husband fakes

being sick so he can stay home and make love to his wife all day, you have to call his team and let them know he won't be going to work."

She was laughing as he ran into the cabin carrying her.

* * * * *